The Dark Side of the Moon

Richard L. Smith

ISBN: 978-1-7371314-3-4

This work is a book of fiction. Names of characters within are fictitious, except for astronomer Mike Brown who is a real person. The geology and names of places on the backside of the Moon are factual as is the science in this book.

Other Books
by Richard L. Smith

Time Lacuna	2003	1ˢᵗ Books
Out of China	2005	Xulon
New Eden	2009	iUniverse
Powerless	2011	iUniverse
Sedna	2016	Publishwholesale
Little Church in the Wilderness	2017	Publishwholesale

Contents

Preface

W hy, you may ask, is the name of this novel *The Dark Side of the Moon*? After all, the farside of the Moon is not dark; it receives as much sunlight every two weeks as the front side does. The more proper term is farside of the Moon. The term "dark" is often used in science to denote our lack of knowledge, such as in Dark Matter and Dark Energy. Because the Moon is tidally locked to Earth, we could only see the front side, and so to us the farside was dark. We had no idea what the other side looked like until the Soviet space probe Luna 3 took the first photographs of the farside of the Moon in 1959. When astronomers first viewed these photographs, they were shocked. Mountainous and covered by tens of thousands big and small craters, the backside looked nothing like the front side. Only 2% maria (flat lava plains) that cover much of the nearside are on the backside. It was if the Moon had been slapped together by two totally different processes.

The Apollo 8 astronauts were the first astronauts to see the farside when they orbited the Moon in 1968. Prior to 2019, all manned and unmanned soft landings were on the nearside of the Moon. The first soft landing on the farside was in January 2019 when the Chinese Chang'e 4 spacecraft landed in the Von Kramer Crater and deployed the Yutu-2 rover. They shared high-resolution images of the crater floor and direct analysis of the lunar ejecta and regolith materials.

Encouraged by the Chinese success, astronomers suggested installing a large radio telescope on the farside, where the Moon would shield it from possible radio interference from Earth. American astronomers began lobbying for a new optical telescope and a gravitational telescope to be built on the backside of the Moon.

My novel takes place in the sixth decade of the twenty-first century when new scientific instruments are coming online. Considering the tremendous advancements in astronomy that have taken place in the past fifty years, it is presumptuous to predict what these new instruments might be in the next fifty years, but without that guesswork, there would be no story which follows the career of astronomer Dr. Seth Byrne, an understudy of astronomer Dr. Mike Brown who discovered several Kuiper Belt minor planets including Sedna in the early twenty-first century. He has been appointed as director of the latest telescope, the Lemaitre Synoptic Telescope (LST), part of NASA's Project Farside. The new telescope has been constructed in the crater Daedalus on the backside of the Moon which also houses a radio telescope and a gravitational interferometer telescope. The deployment of the LST is fraught with problems, including sabotage by unknown criminals. How Seth and his team resolve these problems, achieve "first light" with the LST, and explore the universe with these new Project Farside instruments are a major focus of this story. They also explore the Moon so that it becomes less dark.

Chapter One
Planet Nine

April 2067

Seth Byrne opened his eyes and waited for his vision to clear. He felt woozy and disoriented. His surroundings were indistinct and without form. Eventually his brain cleared enough for him to realize that he was alone in a strange bed located in an unfamiliar white room. A catheter attached to his left arm ran up to a bag hanging from a tree rack next to his bed. Wires dangled from his chest and right arm and ended in a rack of computer equipment which emitted an annoying beep every few seconds. Bandages covered his right hand, and the left side of his face felt numb. He mouthed a whisper from his dry lips, "I'm in a damn hospital!"

Seth had no idea why he was in a hospital or how he got here. He tried to recall his last waking moments, but the only thing his brain could recall was that he was driving to work on a Palo Alto city street. Although he felt no pain, he realized that he had no feeling in his legs. He tried to move his left foot which stuck out from under the blanket, but there was no response. After a few minutes, he was aware that someone had entered the room.

"Well, I see that we have come back to the world," he heard a distinctly feminine voice say.

He turned his head to view the source of the voice. A woman in a white uniform stood beside the equipment rack and examined the computer screen display.

"How are we feeling? Do we have any pain?" He didn't answer, but he thought, "Why do nurses always use the pronoun 'we' when there is only one of me laying here in this bed?" The nurse repeated her question, and this time Seth answered, "*We* are feeling like *we* drank a bottle of Scotch and *we* are feeling no pain."

"Just the effect of the morphine you are on," she answered, choosing to ignore his sarcasm.

"Why am I here in this hospital?" Seth asked.

"You were in a bad car accident. You are in Stanford Hospital. I am Betty, your nurse. Dr. Thompson is your doctor, and he will be in momentarily to check up on you."

"How long have I been in this hospital?"

"Two days," Betty answered.

"Two days, two whole days?" he asked.

"Yes, two days," she repeated as she changed the bag hanging from the tree and adjusted the valve. "For the past two days, you were only semiconscious. Dr. Thompson will be pleased that you are now fully conscious and able to answer his questions when he examines you."

Ten minutes later, Dr. Thompson entered the room and introduced himself.

"You were in a bad accident the other day. A young driver was texting when he ran a red light and T-boned your car. You have some facial cuts, a broken hand, a bruised spleen, and a bruised lower back. You should recover from all this trauma in a few days, but right now you probably have no feeling in your legs due to a bruise to your spinal cord in your lower back. Not to worry, feeling should return in a few days."

"How long do you think I will be here?"

"I think only for a few days, until the feeling returns to your legs and you can take a few steps."

Right after Dr. Thompson left the room, Terry, Seth's wife for the past eighteen years, stood next to his bed. Standing beside her was Will, their fifteen-year-old son.

Seth's mood brightened as Terry leaned over and kissed him.

"It is great to see you awake again," she said. "Will and I have been so worried…," her voice trailed off as she choked back a sob.

Seth managed a weak smile. "Dr. Thompson was just here and said I would be here for a few more days."

"I'll be glad to have you home again," Terry said with a reassuring smile.

"And so will I," Will added.

Seth looked at his son William who was now a freshman at Stanford University. *How did this young man grow up so fast*, he thought. *With all my trips to South America, I have really neglected him.* Will squeezed Seth's hand, and they spoke with him for a few more minutes before Terry kissed him and they left with a promise to return tomorrow. Three days later the feeling in his legs had returned, and with the help of crutches, he could walk again. Dr. Thompson discharged him, and Terry drove him to their home in Palo Alto.

*****

Recovering at home, Seth lay on a couch preparing to take an afternoon nap. His mind wandered as he pondered his career and recent successes in his chosen field of astronomy. He had a lot to be proud of.

He earned his PhD from Washington State University, and after six years working at Palomar Observatory, Stanford University hired him as a professor in the Astronomy Department. For the past six years, he has been a tenured professor in the Astronomy Department of Stanford University in Palo Alto, California. Inspired by his famous mentor and prize-winning astronomer Dr. Mike Brown, Seth became a member of the Kuiper Belt Advanced Research Project or KBARP whose main mission was to discover trans-Neptune objects. Convinced of the existence of a ninth planet, Seth had spent eight unfruitful years searching for the elusive planet which he calculated would orbit at the extreme limits of the Kuiper Belt. When Mike Brown began his search, Pluto was the largest known member of this trans-Neptunian belt known as the Kuiper Belt. In his years as founder of KBARP, Dr. Brown discovered several Kuiper Belt dwarf planets including his discovery of Sedna, Eris, and several other dwarf planets. Yet his main objective remained to discover the ninth planet. The evidence Dr. Mike Brown relied on for what was then called "Planet Nine" came from the other Kuiper Belt minor planets whose orbits were skewed by the gravitation of a large planet circling way beyond the orbits of Neptune and Pluto and even Sedna. This planet would influence the orbits of other Kuiper Belt minor planets that Mike studied. Planet Nine was predicted to be a very distant and massive planet, many times the mass of Earth. Despite years of searching, Planet Nine remained elusive and enigmatic for Dr. Brown. After he retired in 2024, Mike handed the KBARP team leadership to his associate, Dr. Dennis Friedman. The team including Seth continued to search the Kuiper Belt for other objects, and their efforts were rewarded with the discovery of the largest known Kuiper Belt minor planet ever found, a minor planet larger than Pluto or Eris. This newly discovered minor planet orbited seventy-five astronomical units (AU) beyond the Sun, or seventy-five times further away from the Sun than Earth is. The International Astronomical Union (IAU) named this discovery Tesla. Even though Tesla was larger than our Moon, it did not clear its orbit of material and thus did not qualify as a planet. Instead, it was listed as another dwarf planet. Tesla was too small to be the elusive Planet Nine, but this discovery brought Seth international fame and in 2027 a Nobel Prize for his discovery of the dwarf planet Tesla, yet Tesla was not the primary object of Seth's research. He knew that Planet Nine was still out there, and he and his team were going to discover it.

Seth further recalled that the day after his team's discovery of Tesla, he took a celebratory overnight camping trip with his friend and fellow KBARP astronomer Kip Wheeler. Together they traveled on the Atacama Desert floor surrounding the Los Campanas Observatory and set up camp about five miles away from the observatory. At an altitude of 8,500 feet, the desert air was not only thin but drove a cold chill deep into the camper's bodies. After erecting their dome tents, they gathered some sticks and started a bonfire. As they sat around the fire and shared bottle of twenty-year-old Scotch, Kip pointed to a bright light he saw rising over a 14,000 foot mountain to the east. "What is that?" Kip asked.

"Probably a satellite," Seth answered.

As they watched, the light made its way across the sky from east to west until, when overhead, it came to a complete stop.

"That's no satellite," Kip cried out.

The light hovered overhead for a few seconds and then grew larger and brighter as it approached the Los Campanas Observatory perched on a prominence above the desert floor. After another few seconds, a visible disk was discernible, and the object seemed to stop right over the observatory where it remained for a minute or so and then shot straight up and out of sight.

"My God" Kip exclaimed. "I think we just saw a UFO."

"We did," Seth answered. "I have never before witnessed a UFO. The Atacama Desert is infamous for reports of UFO sightings, and now we know that some of these reports are real."

Kip thought for a moment and then said, "I have been a skeptical of UFO sightings and chalked them up to satellites, or airplanes, or perhaps meteorites. Some others say it is just due to active imaginations or too much Scotch. But what we saw was none of these things, and we hadn't had that much Scotch. I have to admit that at least some of these sightings must be real."

In 2028 Dr. Dennis Freedman and his KBARP team were awarded time on the new 24.5-meter Giant Magellan Telescope (GMT). The GMT was ideally suited for the task of discovering trans-Neptune minor planets, and Seth anticipated that with this new instrument, he could find and gather data on Planet Nine. In late 2028, the KBARP team finally found the elusive Planet Nine at the extreme edge of our solar system, 100 billion miles from the Sun. Seth confirmed the position, the orbit, and the mass but could not image the planet. The IAU promptly named the ninth planet Janus, the two-faced Roman God who is looking both backward and forward at the same time. As the computers had predicted, Janus was a massive planet, eleven times the mass of Earth. It orbited the Sun with a perihelion of 1,310 astronomical units (AUs) and aphelion of 189 AUs, and its orbit was skewed 34 degrees to the ecliptic. It would take Janus 21,500 years to complete one orbit around the Sun, but each time it approached the Sun, it effected the orbits of several Kuiper Belt objects. At the time of its discovery, it was at 894 AUs and its magnitude of 23.5 and distance from the ecliptic explained why it was so difficult to locate and identify this object.

Despite its size and light-capturing ability, the GMT telescope could only image Janus as a pinhead-size disk but did confirm its 13,000-mile diameter. The tool that he needed was a high-resolution telescope unencumbered by the Earth's distorting atmosphere. When the James Webb Space Telescope failed to perform as promised, Seth began lobbying NASA for a large telescope on the backside of the Moon.

*****

After Seth awoke from his nap in Palo Alto, he called his boss, Dr. Nye, at Stanford University.

"I am glad to hear about your recovery. When can you return to work?" Dr. Nye asked.

"Next Monday," Seth said.

"That's great. We will all glad to see you again. Dr. Ron Smithers at NASA has been calling you about Project Farside. He left his cell phone number and wants you to contact him as soon as possible," Dr. Nye said.

"I will do so immediately," Seth promised.

To be a part of Project Farside was a dream that he had for some years and one that he must now reconsider.

Dr. Ron Smithers was the director of NASA's Project Farside. Impressed by Seth's resume and his discovery of several other Kuiper Belt minor planets including Sedna and Tesla, Ron had made an offer for Seth to join Project Farside on the farside of the Moon as director of the Lemaitre Observatory that housed the new Lemaitre Synoptic Telescope. Seth initially declined the position, but initially Seth declined the offer because it required a commitment of two years away from Earth and home. Seth's fifteen-year-old son, Will, was entering Stanford as a freshman, and his Dad's long absences away at the GMT in South America and now a proposed two-year absence on the Moon would further deprive Will of his dad's guidance. These would be years with his son that Seth could never recover. Yet this offer from Dr. Smithers tugged on him, and his recent accident had caused him to rethink Ron's offer. Seth was satisfied with his present position at Stanford and felt that Janus' discovery vindicated his mentor who was accused by some as "the Pluto planet killer." Dr. Michael Brown's Kuiper Belt discoveries in the first decade of the twenty-first century initiated a heated discussion among IAU members. Should Pluto and other small objects such as Ceres be reclassified as dwarf planets? Many Kuiper Belt objects like Pluto and Eris are round and orbit the Sun, yet each are smaller than our Moon. So, if they are considered as planets, are there nine, ten, or a dozen planets in our solar system? The IAU settled the question by placing a third requirement necessary to classify a body as a planet. The object must also clear its orbit of all material. Lacking the third requirement, the IAU voted to demote Pluto and reclassify Ceres and other trans-Neptune objects as minor or dwarf planets. This angered many Pluto admirers who disagreed with the International Astronomical Union's conclusion and vented their anger on Dr. Michael Brown whose participation in the discovery of large Kuiper Belt bodies such as such as Sedna, Makemake, Eris, Quaoar, and other Pluto-size trans-Neptune objects had initiated this classification argument.

"Dr. Brown had nothing to do with the declassification of Pluto," Seth often complained. "That was the IAU's doing. His daughter used to chide him that he should find this missing planet so folks would forget that he had a hand in demoting Pluto."

Seth felt his mission to restore his mentor's name had not yet been fully achieved. Managing a telescope capable of studying Janus would certainly go a long way in doing so. Now Seth had an opportunity to become a part of the most exciting new observatory in years, one capable of studying Janus. He picked up his cell phone and called Dr. Ron Smithers at NASA Headquarters in Santa Barbara, California, and said that he had changed his mind and if the offer was still open, he wanted to accept. Ron was thrilled that Seth was now willing to accept his offer.

"Indeed, the offer is still open," Dr. Smithers said. "We very much need you to manage this project. We have spent years and billions of dollars to construct this observatory on the farside of the Moon. First light of the Lemaitre telescope is expected by mid-August. Do you think you could be ready to travel to the Moon six weeks from now?"

"Yes, while I'm still recovering from my accident, I believe I can be ready by next month."

"Well then, meet me at our Santa Barbara NASA facilities forty days from now, and be prepared to travel to the Moon."

Seth ended his call and found Terry in the kitchen.

"I have accepted Dr. Smithers' offer. I'm to meet him at NASA Headquarters in Santa Barbara the middle of July, and I will travel to Project Farside on the Moon the following week."

Terry was used to Seth's long absences on the Atacama Desert, but the prospect of him being on the backside of the Moon where communications were limited upset her.

"How long do you think you will be there?"

"About two years."

"Will we be able to talk to one another?"

"Yes, but it will be limited. There is a Chinese relay satellite parked at the L2 Lagrangian point beyond the Moon which provides service between the backside and Earth for Chang'e 4. The Chinese have leased one channel for Farside use. NASA has also constructed a data relay facility on the South Pole where it has a line of sight on both Earth and Project Farside. Nevertheless, this link is mainly for relaying data, but we can set up a weekly time for me to contact you over the Chinese link."

Seth then called Dr. Nye, the dean of the Stanford University Astronomy Department, and explained his new NASA assignment. He resigned from the Kuiper Belt Advanced Research Project and requested a leave of absence as a tenured professor at Stanford University. Two days later Dr. Nye called him back and said that the University had approved his request and wished him Godspeed in his new assignment.

Chapter Two
Project Farside

Ever since the late 2020s, funding for astronomy had declined. The US Congress and the EAU felt that public funds were better spent on other sciences and social programs. Those opposed to astronomy in general and specifically to exoplanet research gained the upper hand claiming, "Even if we should find an Earth-like planet out there, so what? It would take a multi-billion-dollar probe several centuries to get to the nearest star system to search for life. It is not a priority."

After the orbiting observatory, Transiting Exoplanet Survey Satellite (TESS) completed its mission in 2023 and found dozens of other solar system planets in the habitual zones of nearby stars, funding for new astronomical instruments waned. Coupled with the failure of the James Webb Space Telescope to meet its objectives in 2023, money for deep-space exploration all but dried up. For the next twenty-five years, astronomy was preempted by social and infrastructure programs. No new telescopes were on the drawing boards, and the only ongoing space programs were those already funded such as a probe to Eris and another to Sedna. Due to the cost of the Mars spaceship, the Man on Mars program ended in 2034 with no human sent to Mars.

By mid-century, most attitudes in the USA toward funding for astronomy began to change and Congress not only approved funding for another probe to Pluto but also for a mission to Neptune's large moon, Triton. Astronomers needed a deep-space telescope but one that, unlike the James Webb, could be serviced and upgraded. Since NASA had successfully built the Horizon Moon Base on the Moon's nearside, an observatory on the backside of the Moon gained favor.

After years of lobbing NASA and Congress, Seth and his colleges received funding in 2049 for the design of the Lemaitre Synoptic Telescope to be built on the backside of the Moon as part of the ambitious Project Farside. The 12-meter diameter LST and observatory was scheduled for "first light" in August 2067. The design of the LST was based on the Greek word "synopsis" that refers to looking at all aspects of something. The LST was synoptic in several ways: When operating during the two-week-long Moon night, LST could capture data on millions of objects in six wavelengths. The Project Farside would not only house the LST but also two other observatories, the Penzias-Wilson Radio Telescope (PWRT) and the Einstein Gravitational Wave Observatory (EGWO). The backside of the Moon was an ideal place to locate the Project Farside. Unfettered by interference from Earth, the LST together with the two other Farside projects PWRT and EGWO could capture an unprecedented amount of RF data on deep-space objects and use astronomy's newest instrument to study gravitational waves at greater resolution. In 2053 Congress approved funding for all three Farside projects. The LST observatory would provide advantages over terrestrial or even optical space telescopes. Not only was there no atmosphere to disrupt seeing, but because the observatory will be inside the Earth's shadow, it will enjoy the darkest local sky possible. Unencumbered by Earth's radio noise, the 500-foot PWRT will be the largest operating radio telescope in service and in 2066 became the first operational instrument at Farside. The EGWO was the most sensitive gravitational instrument ever constructed with each 90-degree arm extending 30 kilometers. EGWO and the 500-meter-wide radio telescopes could only be practical in the one-eighth gravity of the Moon.

The Farside Observatory took five years to construct and first light was expected in 2067. The LST was a multiwavelength telescope designed to study immediate and deep-space wavelengths and to search for habitable planets orbiting other star systems. The LST had two primary objectives: to resolve and gather multiwavelength data on exosolar planets and to resolve and study the Kuiper Belt and the ninth planet, Janus. The Farside Base was initially scheduled for completion in 2062but trying to build a base on the airless backside of the Moon proved more daunting and expensive than initially thought. The Farside Base finally became operational in 2065 and the Penzias-Wilson Radio Telescope and Einstein Gravitational Wave Observatory went online that same year. Construction of the LST at Farside began in 2065 with first light scheduled two years later. The LST was ideally designed to meet the need for a wide-field, extended wavelength telescope, and the astronomical community anxiously waited for the new telescope to go online. Although Planet Nine had been discovered and its distance and orbit verified, only the mass and diameter of planet Janus were known. Its remaining physical properties were only educated guesses. No telescope on Earth or in space could resolve Janus and gather critical data. Janus was 894 AUs from the Sun, fifteen times further away than little Sedna which Seth's mentor had also discovered sixty years earlier. None of the existing space or ground-based telescopes were powerful enough to resolve Janus, but the LST at Farside Observatory should be able to do so. Seth felt honored to follow his mentor's career and join the Project Farside to study Janus.

Daedalus Crater

Chapter Three
The Backside of the Moon

July 2067

Seth and Terry drove to San Jose, the terminus of the Coastal Maglev train to Santa Barbara. He kissed Terry goodbye, boarded the train, and arrived in Santa Barbara two hours later. Seth took a cab to the NASA Headquarters in downtown Santa Barbara where he found Dr. Smithers' office and knocked on the door.

"Come in," a friendly voice beckoned. Seated behind a large oak desk covered by stacks of papers and surrounded by shelves of books sat Dr. Ron Smithers, director of the Project Farside, a pleasant looking middle-aged overweight man sporting a generous mustache. He wore a smile and a bright blue tie tucked inside of a white lab coat.

Dr. Smithers stood up and warmly greeted Seth. After a vigorous handshake, he said, "Welcome to Project Farside and please have a seat." He then explained about Seth's new job and the project that he was soon to manage. He began with a brief history of exploration on the backside of the Moon.

"After three Chinese Chang lander and rover missions landed on the farside of the Moon, in 2032 NASA finally sent their Surveyor 10 mission to the Moon's backside. For the next twenty years, world governments curtailed their Moon missions and refocused their limited resources on solving problems on Earth. Because of the success of USSF's Horizon Moon Base on the nearside of the Moon and the disappointment of the James Webb Space Telescope, by mid-century NASA approved funding for a radio telescope, gravitational telescope, and optical observatory on the backside of the Moon and initiated Project Farside."

Dr. Smithers activated a holographic projector that displayed a 3D projection of the Moon that appeared to hang in midair. He rotated the moon to expose the backside and then zoomed in to a large crater named Daedalus.

"Located near the center of the backside of our moon is the fifty-mile-wide Daedalus Crater whose flat floor and terraced crater walls rise over a mile high. A 300-meter-high outcrop called the central peak dominates the crater floor. The Daedalus Crater is named after <u>Daedalus</u> of <u>Greek myth</u>. It was first pictured in a famous photograph taken by the <u>Apollo 11</u> astronauts. Originally called "Crater 308" (this was a temporary <u>IAU</u> designation that preceded the establishment of farside lunar nomenclature), the IAU settled on the name Daedalus. Nearby craters of note include <u>Icarus</u> to the east and <u>Racah</u> to the south. Less than a crater diameter to the north-northeast is <u>Lipskiy</u>."

Dr. Smithers zoomed further in to reveal details of Daedalus and its central peak and then zoomed in even further to display the Project Farside Base.

"The Project Farside Base houses three independent observatories, namely, the Lemaitre Observatory, the Penzias-Wilson Radio Telescope, and the Einstein Gravitational Wave Observatory. Dr. Peter Perkins is the director of the Farside Moon Base. Reporting directly to him are Dr. Martha Benedict, director of the EGWO, and Dr. Francis Tammera, director of the Penzias-Wilson Radio Telescope. You are the director of the Lemaitre Optical Observatory and telescope and will report directly to Dr. Perkins. Nevertheless, please keep me informed with a weekly report." Ron paused for a minute to let all this sink in before continuing.

"You and three new Project Farside employees are scheduled to travel tomorrow on the weekly Farside supply shuttle launched from the US Space Force (USSF) West Coast Space Port at Vandenberg AFB. Your first stop will be at Horizon, the US Space Force base on the nearside of the Moon. Two days later another shuttle will take you to Project Farside where you will meet Dr. Perkins. A team of twenty-five Astronomers and fifty-four technicians serving the three observatories already reside at the Farside Base. Dr. Tammera and his team and Dr. Benedict and her team have managed their observatories since 2065."

He used a laser pointer to indicate the features of Farside. "All three observatories have their data centers housed here in this building attached to the dome. The forty-meter-wide domed building in the center of the base houses the Lemaitré telescope. The dome is a self-supporting transparent half-globe with no visible supporting structures. The two buildings attached to the dome are the igloo-shaped hangar and the observatory control center. The other building some distance away is the fusion reactor blockhouse. The large dish that dominates the northern part of the complex is the Penzias-Wilson Radio Telescope constructed inside of a small crater about 2.5 kilometers from the dome. A small building some distance from the observatory houses the interferometer for the Einstein Gravitational Wave Observatory. Attached to the building are two thirty-kilometer-long interferometer arms spaced ninety degrees apart." Ron turned off the projector.

"The LST is scheduled to achieve first light on August 13. Once at Farside Base, you will have the privilege of directing that major achievement."

"This will be a new adventure for me," Seth said. "I've never been in space before." Seth's voice sounded a bit apprehensive.

Dr. Smithers smiled and reassured him. "Space travel today is common and no more involved than taking a ride on the Maglev train. I expect the journey to the Moon will take only six hours."

They shook hands, and Ron said, "Have a good trip and the best of luck to you in your new job. I will be looking forward to your reports."

The following day Seth checked into the USSF launch facilities at Vandenberg where he met his three Project Farside companions, Dr. Vince Germain, a fellow astronomer assigned to Project Farside, and Mark and Hector, technicians hired by Project Farside. Seth and his companions were outfitted with space suits including helmets, gloves, and boots. Space suits had evolved into simple attire, as comfortable to wear as a business suit. The transparent helmet was normally carried in a backpack attached firmly to the suit collar. A small oxygen container, recirculating equipment, and a laptop computer also fit into the backpack.

The spacecraft shuttle was scheduled to leave at noon for the Horizon Moon Base. At 11:45 Seth and his three companions and eight other passengers were strapped into their shuttle seats and then treated to a five-minute emergency lecture from steward. Exactly at noon the rocket launched into space and attained Earth orbit in ten short minutes. He did not find the 6-g's experienced during the launch as disconcerting as he found the weightlessness once in orbit. He felt a bit queasy. Other than a fast elevator or parachuting from an airplane, he had never experienced being weightless. It was not a pleasant feeling, and despite the medication he received in preflight, he searched the seat pocket for that familiar white bag should it become necessary. Seth enjoyed a view of Earth on the view screen embedded in the backside of the seat in front of him. As the shuttle orbited over Europe, Asia, and the wide Pacific Ocean, soon a view of the West Coast of America filled the screen. When the California coast came into view, he recognized the San Francisco Bay Area. After two orbits they left Earth and headed toward the Moon. Seth watched the familiar blue orb grow smaller and smaller until the view screen switched to the Moon that lay directly ahead. Accustomed to seeing high-resolution pictures of the Moon or the nearside through his own six-inch refactor telescope, the clarity of the craters now on screen along with distinct topographical features mesmerized him. The Moon was in its quarter phase, so the contrast between sunlight features and the resulting shadows enhanced the view. Five hours later they orbited the Moon fifty miles above the surface. They made two passes over the farside now only partly lit by the Sun. Seth located the Daedalus Crater, but it was too dark to see the Farside Base.

On the next pass over the nearside, they came in for a landing at the Horizon Moon Base spaceport. Seth expected to see several structures, but there wasn't very much that he could identify as a moon base. The only buildings were a large dome-shaped building that looked like an overgrown igloo, a solitary blockhouse, and an acre of solar panels. The shuttle steward said that blockhouse contained the fusion reactor and the igloo was the spaceport's hangar and entrance to the underground facilities. In front of the half-dome igloo was large hangar door and paved landing pad. Responding to Seth's comment that there wasn't very much to see, the steward said that the Moon Base Control Center was 6,500 meters below the surface. Seth didn't even feel a bump as they landed on the spaceport ramp, yet the return of partial gravity told him that they were now on the surface. The igloo hangar door slowly opened to reveal the hangar airlock. The mechanized ramp then carried the shuttle inside the airlock, and after the outside door closed, the airlock was pressured. Everyone was told to unstrap and remain in their space suits but carry their backpack and exit the shuttle. They waited on the ramp until a large metal door leading into the hanger opened. They then proceed inside where several shuttles and moon buggies were parked. Several mechanics were busy servicing one of the shuttles. Three double-wide doors at the back of the hangar marked the elevators that would whisk them to the Control Center far below. Two lights above the doors glowed red, but the middle door light was green. A young lady standing next to the middle door introduced herself as Janet Finch, their Horizon Moon Base tour guide. She led the passengers and shuttle crew inside the elevator and then pushed a red button. Seth was just getting accustomed to the pull of the Moon's weak gravity when he suddenly again became weightless as the elevator dropped at breakneck speed toward the buried Moon Base Control Center. Two minutes later it slowed down and came to a gentle stop. They climbed off the elevator into a locker room where they could take off and store their space suits. That done the outside door opened, and everyone climbed out onto a platform that overlooked a huge cavern that housed the entire well-lit city called Moon Base Control Center. Daylight seemed to emanate from the entire roof and walls of the cavern. Janette explained that the Center had been constructed inside of a natural lava tube 430 feet high, 1200 feet wide, and perhaps a mile long. The so-called Center consisted of a two-dozen block-like four-story buildings, obviously designed for utility rather than architectural aesthetics. Seth noted that these buildings had few windows and asked Janet why this was so.

"No need for windows," she said. "All one would see is the next building or the uninteresting walls and roof of the lava tube."

Janette explained that the large tank just beyond the last of the buildings served as the city water storage facility. She said that the largest of the buildings housed a hydroponic garden which produced all the fresh food for the Center inhabitants. In the center of the city was a park with green grass, flowering bushes, and small fruit trees.

"Water is not a problem at Horizon," Janet explained. "All our water is melted from ice located in a crater near the south pole of the Moon."

She led them downstairs to a central building where she said overnight accommodations for Seth and his companions had been arranged. Then she took them inside to the auditorium where she explained the functions of the Horizon Moon Base. She concluded by saying that tomorrow morning a shuttle had been arranged to take Seth and his three companions to the Farside Base and then took them to the cafeteria where they had dinner and then retired for the night.

The next morning Seth, Vince, Mark, and Hector ate breakfast and returned with Janette to the locker room, donned their space suits, and then rode the elevator back to the surface where the shuttle to Project Farside patiently waited for them. The flight to the backside of the Moon took only forty-five minutes, and soon they were hovering above the Daedalus Crater. The Project Farside was located directly below toward the western crater wall and south of the central mountain peaks. Unlike the Horizon Moon Base, Project Farside consisted of several buildings, the largest of which was the forty-meter diameter transparent dome of the Lemaitre Observatory. Inside of a small crater, a mile from the observatory spread the 500-meter wide Penzias-Wilson Radio Telescope. Located a few hundred meters north of the Farside Observatory sat another building with two protruding arms, the Einstein Gravitational Wave Observatory. The shuttle slowly descended toward another igloo spaceport identical to the Horizon Base spaceport. Once they had landed on the ramp, the airlock door opened, and the platform and shuttle moved inside. Once the airlock was repressured, the main hangar door opened, and they were instructed to deplane and bring their backpacks with them. A young lady dressed in a Project Farside uniform met them at the foot of the shuttle door and introduced herself as Sally Elmhurst and shook hands with Seth and the other passengers.

"I have been assigned as Dr. Byrne's assistant and will be your tour guide today," she announced with a warm smile and asked them to take off their space suits. Each passenger hung the space suits and their backpacks inside individual lockers marked with their names and dressed in Farside uniforms. A double green door at the back of the hangar was marked "Observatory," and a second door was labeled "Operations Center." A green light over the Operations Center door indicated it was ready to take them to the Center 2,500 feet below. The elevator ride to the Center was gentle, taking a full two minutes to descend. When the elevator door finally opened, they were treated to their first view of the Project Farside Operations Center. The Center cavern was much smaller than the lava tube at the Horizon Moon Base Center. Sally said that the cavern was 260 feet wide and 450 feet long, with a ceiling 97 feet high. The entire cavern was flooded with a bright light that seemed to emanate from the ceiling.

Sally explained, "Because the mantle on the backside of the Moon is thirty miles thicker than that on the nearside, there has been little volcanic activity on the surface. Although covered by impact craters both large and small, the backside is mountainous with few gullies and cracks. Without volcanoes from which lava could flow onto the surface, there is no mare or rift valleys. Since there are no lava tubes in which to construct a base, we had to construct this cavern blasted out of solid rock. The backside remains quite different than the surface that astronomers expected to find here fifty years ago."

In the middle of the Center complex was a park complete with grass, flowering bushes, small ornamental trees, and a small pond. Two five-story block-like windowless buildings were located on opposite sides of the park, and Seth counted six smaller buildings that bordered park perimeter.

A tall, thin gentleman with a well-trimmed beard and dressed in a white lab coat stood on the platform ready to greet them. He introduced himself as Dr. Peter Perkins, the director of Project Farside Moon Base. He first shook hands with Vince, Mark, and Hector and finally stood in front of Seth.

"Welcome to Project Farside and the Lemaitre Observatory, Dr. Byrne," Dr. Perkins said as he offered Seth a wimp, unenthusiastic handshake.

"Tomorrow at 10am I have arranged for a meeting between you and me in my L2 office. I will explain Farside protocol and your duties as the LST director. While here Miss Elmhurst will act as your tour guide and has also been assigned as your personal assistant."

With that short introduction and without further pleasantries or even a "have a good day," he turned and climbed down from the platform and disappeared into the first building.

"A rather humorless abrupt fellow, this director," Vince whispered to Seth.

Sally overheard Vince's comment and blushed. Ignoring the comment, she suggested, "Well then, let's begin our tour," and led them down the steps onto the Center floor. The first stop was the park, where Sally gathered everyone around her and explained the function of each building that surrounded the park.

"The large windowless buildings on our right are L2 which is the main office building and houses the dining hall and movie theater. The other large building across the park is L1 which contains the equipment facilities, the labs, the pool and exercise room, and the hydroponic garden. Offices and labs are on the upper floors. The other buildings around the park are living quarters. The building next to L2 is named Maxwell which contains the cafeteria, a lounge, meeting rooms, and employee bedrooms. Administrator offices are located on the third floor of L2. Dr. Perkins' office is on the second floor with all the other director's offices, including your office, Dr. Byrne. I will take you to L2 next. The living quarters for Dr. Byrne and Dr. Germain are on the second floor of Maxwell. The bedrooms for Mark and Hector are in the employee quarters which is the two-story building behind Maxwell."

The center of the L2 lobby housed a botanical garden with jungle plants that reached up to the second floor. It took up most of the ground floor. The rest of the lobby contained a large reception desk and a generous well-appointed lounge. Next to the lounge was a double door marked "auditorium." The elevator took them to the second floor where Sally pointed out Dr. Perkins' office, and two doors further down the hall, a door marked "Dr. Seth Byrne, Lemaitre Director."

They went inside that office which opened to an anteroom with several comfortable chairs and a reception desk.

"This is my desk," Sally said with a warm smile. A placard on top of the desk announced, "Sally Elmhurst, Assistant to Dr. Byrne." Four chairs and a table with a coffee machine and cups completed the anteroom furnishings.

Seth entered his office and looked around. The floor was covered by a colorful area rug. A large oak desk and adjustable chair sat against the back wall underneath a large photograph of the Hubble Ultra-Deep Field. In front of the desk were two comfortable chairs, and on both walls on either side of the desk were four empty bookshelves.

"My books should arrive next month," Seth mentioned to Sally. Two overstuffed chairs, a couch, and coffee table completed the office furnishings.

Next, Sally took them to the staff meeting room located at the end of the hall. Inside was an oblong oak conference table surrounded by a dozen comfortable chairs. A long table alongside one wall completed the room.

They returned to the lobby and the tour next continued to L1, the building directly across the park. They entered the lobby and took the elevator to the third floor where Seth and Vince's living quarters were located. Each bedroom was designed for comfort, with a lounge chair, desk and chair, and single bed. A wide window looked onto the park below and a large TV screen covered one wall.

The next stop was the ground floor lounge. The hydroponic garden, pool, and exercise rooms were also on the ground floor. The second floor was devoted to labs filled with lab benches and analytical equipment. The tour went on to the building next door to L1 called Maxwell.

By now Seth was hungry, so they stopped at the Maxwell cafeteria for lunch. After lunch Sally took them back to the L1 auditorium where she showed a 3D holographic film depicting the history and layout of the Project Farside facilities. After her presentation, the tour ended. Seth retired to his bedroom for some needed rest before the newcomers met with Sally for dinner at 6pm in the L2 dining hall. Seth slept well that evening, arose at 7am, and met Vince in the Maxwell cafeteria for a planned breakfast. At 9:30 he left for his 10am appointment with Dr. Perkins. After waiting in Dr. Perkins' outer office, precisely at 10am, his assistant ushered Seth into the inner office where Dr. Perkins sat at his desk perusing a stack of paperwork. When Seth entered, and without speaking or rising, Dr. Perkins waved his hand for Seth to take a seat in front of his desk. Seth sat down and waited but the director continued to peruse his paperwork. After a couple of minutes, he pushed the papers aside and without saying a word stared at Seth. It was a cold and unsmiling stare. Finally, he leaned forward and for the first time spoke.

"I see by your resume that you graduated with a BS in physics from Santa Clara University and obtained your MS and PhD in astronomy from Washington State University. Neither of these universities are renowned for their astronomy departments."

Seth bristled at the remark yet said nothing.

Peter continued, "Nevertheless, you are a tenured professor at Stanford University and a member of the Kuiper Belt Advanced Research Project. As such you have been credited with the discovery of the minor planet Tesla and there is talk about a Noble Prize. While the discovery of Tesla was a major accomplishment, I believe it was due to dumb luck rather than in-depth science."

This remark caught Seth completely off guard, but he felt compelled to respond to this unfounded charge.

"Many discoveries in science like that of super glue are due to dumb luck, but my team's discovery of Tesla was the result of careful research and determined perseverance. There is a lot of empty space out there, and knowing where to search for Tesla was the result of years gathering data and plotting the orbits of several other Kuiper Belt objects. This discovery was the result of thorough science and perseverance, and not as you say, 'dumb luck.' I take your remarks as a personal insult. Do you have a problem with me?"

Surprised at Seth's response, Dr. Perkins leaned back in his chair. "To be honest, I really do not understand your appointment as director. You have had no direct involvement in the design and construction of the Lemaitre Observatory and telescope. This puts you at a disadvantage as the director of Lemaitre. I don't know what Ron was thinking when he appointed you. You will have a lot to learn about Farside and the synoptic telescope. As director of the Lemaitre

Observatory, you will report directly to me, and I expect to be completely informed about the status of the LST."

"Understood," Seth said.

Dr. Perkins then handed Seth a two-page brochure. "This will explain the rules and protocol for the Farside Moon Base operations. I fully expect that you and any staff that you may appoint will remain in full compliance with these rules."

Seth glanced through the brochure and stared back at Peter. After a minute of uncomfortable silence, Dr. Perkins finally said, "I'm sure you are anxious to visit the observatory and tour that operation. You are excused to do so."

Completely bewildered by the tone of this first meeting and the arrogance of Dr. Perkins, Seth rose and walked out of the office.

When he returned to his office, he asked Sally if he had had any calls. She said no, but she could see that he was visibly upset. "The meeting with Dr. Perkins did not go well?"

"Not at all."

She did not seem surprised. "Dr. Perkins has a reputation of being rather abrupt, especially in a first meeting. I'm sure as he gets to know you better, he will mellow."

"Can you take me to the observatory? I would very much like to see the telescope."

"No problem," Sally said.

Chapter Four
First Light

S ally and Seth took the elevator back to the surface hangar and approached the green door marked "Observatory."

"Look into the facial recognition eye," Sally said. There was a soft click, the door slid open, and Sally and Seth walked out onto the floor of the observatory. It was still nighttime on the backside, so the observatory was bathed in a soft red light.

Seth's first impression was that the observatory was huge, and although he knew that a forty-meter dome covered the observatory, it looked as if he was outside and could reach up and touch the stars that shone from the firmament above.

Sally noticed Seth gazing upward and explained about the dome.

"Unlike the observatory domes on Earth, a dome on the Moon cannot be opened to the outside vacuum of space. Like a thin soap bubble, this dome is a technological marvel only supported by inside air pressure. The two-millimeter skin of the dome admits 99.7% of the light from IR to UV."

Seth turned his attention to the center of the room occupied by the Lemaitre telescope mounted on a large gantry. The Ritchey-Chretien twelve-meter reflector mounted on a Cardan suspension gimbal allowed the telescope to slew in a matter of a few minutes to anywhere on the celestial sky. Engineers and technicians crawled over the gantry making last-minute adjustments and tests in preparation for first light, now only a week away. A one-meter secondary mirror was suspended at the focal point above the primary mirror. Unlike the picture of Edwin Hubble peering into the objective of his 100-inch Hooker telescope on Mt. Wilson, no one would be looking directly through this telescope. Light gathered by the primary and secondary mirrors passed through a series of optics and then fed by an optical fiber link to the control room where the various wavelengths are separated and individually recorded and then reconstructed by computer and an enhanced composite picture would appear on an overhead computer screen.

"Come with me. I want to introduce you to Dr. Pamela Hernandez, our principal astronomer," Sally suggested. They climbed up the gantry stairs to the third level where a tall woman with short dark hair dressed in a white lab coat was busy examining gauges on an instrument panel. She saw Sally and her companion coming and stepped away from the instrument panel.

"Hello Sally, and this must be Dr. Seth Byrne," Pamela said as she smiled and extended a hand to Seth. "I'm so glad to finally meet you. Welcome to the LST." Pamela's smile was as warm as her handshake was friendly and firm.

"Dr. Hernandez, I am honored to meet you," Seth said as they shook hands. Seth seemed reluctant to release her hand.

"Please, I am better known around here as Pam," she said.

"Then, Pam it will be," Seth promised. "I'll bet you are excited about 'first light' next week."

"After years of hard work, we all are. It is so exciting that you could be here with us to celebrate this monumental achievement."

"I'll let you get back to work, but I would like to invite you to my first staff meeting at 10am Friday morning in the staff meeting room on the second floor of L2."

"I'll be there along with Dr. Bruce Elderly, my lead astronomer, and Dr. Bess Martin, our LST software engineer," Pam said.

On the main floor of the observatory, Seth met the lead LST project engineer, Jim Karnowski, who had Vince and Mark with him. Seth said hello to his travel companions and then shook hands with Jim and asked him some questions about the LST. Jim explained a few technical details about the operation of the telescope and gimbal mount. He said that a small spotter scope located at the LST Annex on the rim of Daedalus Crater twenty-six miles away allowed them to accurately position LST. He then introduced Seth to several other technicians and engineers.

"We have a staff of twenty-five technicians, engineers, and computer programmers at Farside to service the LST. The LST is an extraordinarily complex instrument that takes a large staff to service and maintain all the software, computers, and mechanical and optical equipment," Jim explained.

Seth also invited Jim and Pete Fulmer, the lead mechanical project engineer, to his staff meeting.

The next stop was to the LST, EGWO, and PWRT control rooms, housed in the separate building adjacent to the main LST floor. Three doors, one painted yellow, one green, and another blue, were each guarded by their own security scanner. Sally stood in front of the blue door marked "LST Control Room" and peered into the scanner. The door slid open with a whisper and she then led Seth inside.

The control room was smaller than Seth imagined and reminded him of the control room at the Vandenberg launch facilities. Arranged in a semicircle were a dozen desks, each equipped with high-resolution wide-screen computers. A 100-inch 3D view screen mounted to one wall and visible to everyone occupied one wall of the control room. The view on the screen was that of the Earth as it would appear from 20,000 miles.

"The LST spectrum optics captures everything from IR to UV, but the large overhead screen will display a visual composite picture constructed from all wavelengths," Sally explained. She introduced Seth to each of the astronomers and engineers manning the individual desk. He also met Bess Martin and her software team and invited her to his weekly staff meeting. Seth asked each person about their function and then asked a few technical questions of each.

"Next, we should visit the radio telescope control room adjacent to this one," Sally suggested. The yellow door was marked "Penzias-Wilson Control Room." The inside of this room was even smaller than that of the LST control room. A dozen screens, oscilloscopes, and gauges covered one wall. Four desks, each occupied by an operator, faced the wall. As they entered the room, a small woman in a lab coat stood up, greeted Sally, and held out her hand to Seth and said, "I am Dr. Francis Tammara, director of the radio telescope. Welcome to the PWRT or Penzias-Wilson Radio Telescope."

Seth took her small, thin hand into his and gently squeezed it. Her thin tapered hand reminded him of one belonging to a concert pianist.

"I'm very pleased to meet you as well Dr. Tammara," Seth said.

"Please, just call me Tess," she pleaded. "Everyone around here does."

"Tess, please tell me a bit about your team, this control room, and what you have been learning with this unique instrument," Seth asked.

Tess broke into a broad smile as she withdrew her hand. She then took him to each desk and introduced him to the operator, who then explained his job and about the data he was collecting.

"At 500 meters diameter, this is the most sensitive radio telescope that NASA owns, and from this very quiet RF location on the backside of the Moon, in only several months of operation, we have gathered more data on Sagittarius A*, the black hole at the center of our galaxy, than has been gathered in the past thirty years," Tess said with obvious pride. "Our telescope can penetrate all the gas and dust surrounding the black hole and allow us to examine the event horizon and surrounding ring of material in detail."

Seth thanked her and said, "I will hold my first staff meeting at 10am Friday morning in the staff meeting room on the second floor of L2. As a fellow director, you are invited to sit in on my first staff meeting and perhaps give us a summary of what is going on with the PWRT." She thanked him and said she would attend.

Their next visit was to the Einstein Gravitational Wave Observatory control room behind the green door.

Sally introduced Dr. Martha Benedict, the EGWO director. A stately woman with a pleasant smile greeted him. Her gray hair and thick glasses suggested that she may be in her sixties. The room was about the same size as the PWRT room with six computer desks arranged in three rows. She took him from desk to desk introducing her staff while explaining the functions of each.

"Several advanced gravitational wave telescopes have been built since LIGO and Virgo, but Einstein is the most sensitive ever constructed. Gravitational wave interferometry has opened a new window on the universe and EGWO is gathering reams of data. Each arm of our interferometer is precisely 90 degrees apart and 30 kilometers long providing 10,000 times more resolution than LIGO," she said. "The interferometer sends a powerful split laser beam down each long arm to a mirror that returns the beams to interfere with each other in the central building about three miles from here. Even a micron difference in the distance traveled down one of the arms will register in the interferometer. EGWO has been operational for past several months, and already we have observed the collision of four black holes and two neutron suns."

"I'm anxious to hear more details about what you have learned in the past few months," Seth said. He then made Martha the same offer to sit in on his first staff meeting.

"Thank you, and I will plan to attend," she promised. "I would also like to meet with you in your office before your next meeting and explain more about the EGWO and my special project to detect Dark Matter."

"I have read your papers about the detection of Dark Matter, and I am anxious to hear what you have learned. Please contact my office manager Sally for an appointment."

After the tour of the control rooms, Sally and Seth returned to his office where he contacted Dr. Vince Germain and asked him to join him for dinner that evening in the small manager's dining room adjacent to the main cafeteria.

As they enjoyed a bottle of wine before ordering dinner, Vince asked, "Well, how did your interview go with Dr. Perkins this morning?"

"Not well," Peter answered. "I left his office profoundly confused."

Vince looked surprised. "What happened?"

"Dr. Perkins was not only unfriendly, but rude and deliberately offensive," Seth said. "He did not hide his irritation with Dr. Smithers for appointing me as the LST director. He thought because I had not participated in the design and construction of the telescope and observatory, I was not qualified to lead this project. He disparaged my degrees earned at Santa Clara and WSU and said that my discovery of the minor planet Tesla was due to dumb luck rather than in-depth science. Then he handed me a Farside Base handbook of regulations and dismissed me. I have never been treated so rudely by a supervisor. All and all, he acted like a pompous ass with a chip on his shoulder."

Vince said nothing for a minute before responding. "While I might understand Dr. Perkins' objection to you as LST director, yet saying this to your face and treating you rudely is beyond the pale. Dr. Perkins is also hypocritical disparaging your degree. His degree is in geology from Northeastern University, and he has no background in astronomy. He came up through the bureaucratic ranks within NASA. I think you should inform Dr. Ron Smithers about this meeting."

"The last thing I want to do is get in the middle of a pissing match between Peter and Ron. I let Dr. Perkins know that I was insulted by his attitude. It is prudent that I just let it pass and try to get along as best I can with him." They enjoyed dinner together and Seth said good night. "Please be my guest at my first staff meeting Friday morning."

On September 11 at 10am, everyone gathered in the control room to watch as the expected preliminary first light appear on the large overhead screen. At first the screen was dark, but then stars began to appear as the software eliminated background scatter. Even though it was not yet completely dark on Daedalus, the view soon filled with stars. The picture zoomed in on the Andromeda constellation and the M-31 galaxy filled the screen. Everyone clapped and cheered their approval. The picture was clear and so sharp that individual stars in M-31 were visible. The next objective was to demonstrate the telescopes' resolving power and display our nearest star system, Alpha Centauri. Its companion stars Alpha Centauri B and Alpha Centauri C, a red dwarf known as Proxima Centauri, were resolved. Proxima's largest satellite was also clearly visible.

Everyone in the control room enthusiastically clapped and yelled their approval. Pam turned around and gave Seth a huge hug. "I'm so glad you were here to witness this historic event," she said wearing a grin that extended from ear to ear. "Now the real work of calibration can begin."

"Congratulations to you and your team," Seth said. You folks have worked so hard for this day. I am proud to be a part of this event. Pam and I will go to Dr. Perkins' office and share the good news with him."

For the first time, Ron greeted them with a smile and then stood up and shook Seth's and Pam's hands when they reported first light. "Now together we will call Dr. Smithers with this great news", he said.

Friday morning Seth met with his staff in the L2 second floor meeting room. Attending were Dr. Pamela Hernandez, Dr. Bruce Elderly, Jim Karnowski, Bess Martin, and Peter Fulmer. His guests were Martha Benedict, Tess Tammera, and Vince Germain. Sally also attended to take notes.

Seth introduced himself and asked each staff member to also give a little history about themselves. Then he asked Pamela for the status of the calibration event scheduled for next week.

Dr. Hernandez reported that they had discovered a problem with the computer memory software. "The LST will capture 100 terabytes of information during each dark sky observation period, and having a reliable memory storage and backup system is critical to the success of this mission. I will let Dr. Martin explain the details."

"During testing we discovered a glitch with the data backup software," Bess said. "The bad news is that we must rewrite and test the corrected version of the software, and this will take ten to fifteen days. I regret to report that we will miss the two-week dark sky window this month and must delay calibration to the dark period in September."

"That is indeed bad news," Seth said. "A lot of folks are anticipating the August 15 calibration date to. Is there anything you can do to speed the rewrite and testing of the software?"

"I doubt it," Bess said. "There are thousands of lines of code that must be rewritten and then extensively tested. My team and I will do everything possible to speed this up, but at this point I don't see how we can be ready by August 15."

After the staff meeting ended, Seth went with Bess down to the LST control room and called an impromptu meeting with the software engineers. He asked again if there was anything, they could do to have the code ready and tested by August 15.

"If we work both day and night, we might be able to rewrite the code, but there wouldn't be adequate time to properly test it by mid-August," Shanduka, the most experienced software engineer on the team, said.

"What could happen if the new code is not thoroughly tested and we just go ahead and hope for the best and implement it?"

Shanduka looked at the hardware engineer Jim Hernandez. "We simply must test it. If there is a flaw in the code, without a working backup system, all the data we collect could be lost. Unfortunately, this testing will take three or four days. A serious flaw could also screw up our memory hardware to the point where much of it would have to be replaced, and that would be catastrophic."

Seth nodded that he understood. "Proceed then and do your best to be ready by the next dark sky window in September."

Seth then ended the meeting and returned to his office.

As soon as he entered, Sally said, "Dr. Perkins called and wants to see you in his office immediately."

Seth went to Peter's office and his secretary immediately ushered him into the inner office.

Peter looked up from his usual pile of papers and waved Seth to take a seat. "I just received some bad news from your LST team," Dr. Perkins said. "A staff member informed me that there would be a two- to three-week delay before calibration could begin."

"This is true," Seth admitted. "I was so informed about the delay at my staff meeting this morning. Something about a software glitch in the memory system."

"This delay is unacceptable," Peter growled. "Everyone back in NASA is expecting calibration next week, and this is what I have promised them. What are you doing to get this problem fixed and the project back on schedule?"

"Unfortunately, a major amount of code must be rewritten and tested which will take time and cause us to miss the dark sky window that ends the third week in August."

Peter slammed his fist hard down on the desk. "There is always something a good manager can do to speed up a process. Have you visited the software team to see what can be done?"

"I have. The new code is complicated. Even if finished in a few days, it still must be tested. This delay will cause us to miss the August dark sky window."

"Well then, insist that Dr. Martin must speed up the testing."

"Testing so much new code is complex, and Dr. Martin and her team told me that they are doing all that is possible to speed up this process."

"Then tell them to damn the testing and just implement the new code," Peter demanded

"Bess and I have discussed this. If the testing is not done and there is an undiscovered glitch inherent in this new software, Jim Hernandez warned me that the main memory hardware could be irreversibly damaged. I am NOT comfortable with a decision to bypass the testing process."

"You are NOT paid to be comfortable," Peter screamed. "Just do it."

"You can either fire me and take over as director of the LST or you could issue a direct order which I will certainly obey. However, it must be in the form of a written order signed and dated by you. Until then I am the director of the LST, and my decision is final."

Peter's face turned scarlet. He knew that Seth had him in a vise. He wasn't about to fire Seth, who had only been on the job for a few days, and he wasn't going to put his signature on a document that would make him fully responsible for any adverse consequences caused by not testing.

"OK then," Peter growled. "Have it your way, but if we are not ready for full operation by the dark sky in September, I'll demand your resignation on my desk."

"We'll be ready, in time for the September dark sky window."

Seth left Peter's office wondering if he could continue to work under this man. It appeared that Dr. Perkins only cared about appearances and did not seem to understand how dangerous his demand would be to the entire project should the new software be flawed. Nevertheless, he had stood his ground even under Peter's unreasonable demands and threats.

Bess Martin proceeded with implementing testing the new software, and as she predicted, her team found not one but three major flaws that if implemented would have damaged Jim's memory hardware. When the flaws were corrected and subsequent testing certified the new code by the end of August, the LST team announced that they were ready for the calibration phase beginning on September 11, the earliest possible date when the Sun will rise on the backside.

Chapter Five
Poltergeist

For the next few days, the LST team continued with the lengthy process of calibrating and fine-tuning the telescope, their instruments, and software. Everything was going as planned until the second week of September when three days from the end of the dark period the telescope suddenly lost its ability to accurately maintain position. That ability was dependent on a spotter scope operating from the LST Annex located on the southern rim of Daedalus twenty-six miles from the Base. Pam reported that without the assistance of the Annex spotter scope, the LST could not accurately find and hold its position on the celestial sphere. The spotter scope would have to be fixed before the calibration and shakedown process could continue, and since there were only two days remaining until daylight on Daedalus returned, unless the spotter scope is immediately fixed, the calibration cannot be concluded and the official start of LST observation will again be delayed until September or October's dark time.

"Peter will be livid at this postponement," Dr. Elderly commented.

"I will have to give him the bad news," Seth said. Pam and Jim went with him to Peter's office and reported that without the spotter scope, LST testing and calibration had come to a sudden halt. The Annex would have to be immediately visited by an engineer qualified to repair the spotter scope. No one on Jim Hernandez's staff was so qualified, so Peter said to contact the NASA LST operations manager in Santa Barbara for help.

As expected, Peter was angry and said, "Just fix the damn spotter scope."

Seth contacted Ron Smithers who promised to immediately send someone from the USSF Moon Base who was intimate with the spotter scope design and operation. Unfortunately, the repair man would take another day to arrive at Farside. In the meantime, the LST was unusable.

That evening Seth was passing through the cafeteria when he spied a familiar face. It was his friend and KBARAK colleague Kip Wheeler. He went over to Kip's table and sat down. "Kip, what in the world are you doing here at Farside?"

Kip looked up from his bowl of chili and broke into a broad smile. "It is great to see you again Seth. I just arrived this afternoon, and after the orientation I stopped by your office to say hello, but you were not there."

"What brings you to Farside Base?" Seth asked.

"I am your spotter scope repairman. I suspect one of the three positioning gyroscopes is at fault, and thanks to the simple design, it will be easy to replace and test any faulty component. Since I helped design this instrument and happened to be visiting the USSF Moon Base, Dr. Smithers asked me to travel to the Farside Base and fix the problem. I intend to travel to the Annex tomorrow. I enjoyed your company on our camping trip to the Atacama Desert years ago, so if you could get away from here for a couple of days, I would very much like for you to accompany me. As director of the LST, it would be beneficial for you to visit the Annex. It's fortunate that it is almost dawn here on the farside because once the scope is fixed, I will be able to test my repair job with the LST both at night and during the day."

"Both fortunate and unfortunate," Seth said, "because there are only three dark days remaining for the LST team to complete calibration. Unless we can immediately fix the spotter scope, we are facing another delay until September or October."

The thought of getting away from the complex and traveling across Daedalus Crater appealed to Seth, so he immediately accepted Kip's offer.

Kip smiled and then continued, "We will be gone for two days. After my repair we will camp out at the spotter scope site to wait for dawn twenty-six hours later. It is also necessary to make sure that my repair is tested over the laser beam that connects Farside with the Annex during both day and nighttime."

The next day, Seth and Kip went to the Farside spaceport prep-room and donned their space suits. A shuttle and three rovers called "moon buggies" sat unattended on the spaceport floor. The moon buggies, each about the size of a buss, were built on tractors and outfitted with small living quarters and a bubble cockpit that would give those inside a full 180-degree view of the land and sky. As they examined the buggies, a third person joined them.

"My name is Dick Puente. I am the electrical engineer in charge of the communications relay station at the Annex, and as a qualified moon buggy driver, I will be your pilot and navigator for this trip. I will also investigate some intermittent problems experienced with the Annex relay station laser transmitter."

Since Farside Base had no direct line of sight with either Earth or the USSF Moon Base, Farside used a series of laser beams between the Annex, the south pole, and the USSF Moon Base. Once each day a Chinese satellite communications probe would be in range, but the Annex laser beams provided a 24/7 link.

They all shook hands and climbed aboard the closest of the three moon buggies, one that had the name "Jenny" painted on its side.

Dick explained a few facts about the moon buggies. "These rovers are fully self-contained, helium and battery-powered machines. It is fully outfitted with oxygen, water, and food sufficient for a three- or four-day journey. Our sojourn across Daedalus to the southern rim base should only take about three or four hours plus another half hour or so to climb up to the summit where the Annex is. It houses the remote spotter telescope and the relay transmitting equipment. After Kip makes the spotter scope repairs and I check out the relay station, we will remain on site for another eighteen hours until dawn so that we can make sure that the telescope is fully functional under a dark and sunlit sky. The buggy will be our home for two full days."

They waited for the outside door to open before Dick started Jenny and headed out of the Farside spaceport. The Sun was not due to rise over the east crater for another twenty-eight hours and Daedalus was still immersed in total darkness. Jenny slowly emerged from the "garage" into the darkened crater, and if not for Jenny's bright headlights, it would not have been possible to see a thing, and Seth was mesmerized by the back glow of the firmament where it looked like he could reach out and touch each individual star. Jenny's headlights pierced the dark crater floor and produced a sharp contrast between the headlights and shadows of the many craters and boulders directly ahead. Jenny lumbered along at ten miles per hour while circumnavigating the numerous small craters and avoiding boulders that peppered the crater floor. After three hours they arrived at the base of the crater rim. Dick searched for the natural ramp that would allow them to access the four terraces that rose from the crater floor to the rim summit. It took the buggy thirty-five minutes to climb up to and cross each terrace and finally arrive at the Annex remote building site. The Annex building and entry garage was larger than Seth had imagined. A one-piece igloo dome roof covered both the spotter scope room and the communications room. Two communication dishes were perched on top of the dome. Part of Dick's mission today was to service the relay station which had experienced some problems. He activated the door of the "garage" airlock and, after it opened, drove Jenny inside. When the door closed, the garage was pressured allowing them to exit the buggy without their helmets. Located at the back of the garage were two doors, each protected by an access lock, a green door marked "FARSIDE RELAY STATION" and a yellow door marked "LST ANNEX." Kip and Seth went inside the LST room while Dick went inside the relay station room. Kip carried an unopened box with a spare gyroscope, and Seth carried a box of test equipment and tools. Kip turned off the tracking scope main power switch and then took the cover off the gyroscope enclosure and peered inside.

"Damn," he exclaimed.

"What's wrong?" Seth asked.

Kip motioned for Seth to come closer.

"Just look at this," he said as he pointed to a power connector for the gyroscopes which lay in two separate parts, a male and a female.

"This interlocked connector that supplies power to all three gyroscopes has been disconnected. It didn't just accidentally disconnect itself. Someone has deliberately disconnected it."

Bewildered, Seth asked, "Who could have done this? No one has visited this site for the past several weeks. The Annex tracking scope was working fine until a few days ago."

"I don't know, but this seems to be the cause of the problem," Kip said. He reconnected the power connector and then turned the main power switch back on. The gyroscopes began to softly hum as they spun up to full speed. Kip took out the test equipment and performed several internal tests.

"Everything now appears to be working properly," Kip claimed.

He contacted Jim Karnowski at the observatory who confirmed that the LST now was online and able to track and hold its position.

Later when all three scientists were back inside Jenny, Kip told Dick about the power connector and asked, "Were any of your transmitter folks recently here at the relay station?"

"No," Dick said. "The moon buggies have not been outside the Base for the past six weeks, so my team could not have visited the Annex. I also found that the computer that runs the relay station had been hacked."

"Hacked?" Kip said

"Yes, hacked. Someone had downloaded a virus timed to activate in six days, thereby disrupting all communications with Earth. This virus could not have been downloaded remotely but can only be downloaded from the computer control panel at the Annex relay site. Thankfully, I was able to remove the virus before it activated."

Kip sighed. "Well then, this is an even deeper mystery. There is no way the connector could have simply disconnected itself. Someone had to be physically there to disconnect the power and from the main panel downloaded a virus. Have there been any new visitors to the Farside Base site in the past two weeks? Could the Chinese have made a visit? The Chinese Science Moon Base named KARMA in the Von Karman Crater is located 700 miles from here, and it is unlikely that those folks could have made a visit."

"No, neither someone from Farside nor the Chinese base made a visit," Dick said. "The Chinese supply ship to the KARMA base was here last month, but it was unlikely to have visited the Annex. It is not scheduled to arrive again until next month. Other than the Chinese supply ship, the only other ship for the past two months on the backside was the shuttle that brought you folks to Farside."

"Perhaps we have a poltergeist at work here," Kip said.

Dick frowned. "A poltergeist?"

"Only joking," Kip quickly added.

Chapter Six
The Sphere

Kip, Dick, and Seth remained at the Annex site for another eighteen hours until the Sun began to rise over the crater rim. Kip made a series of final tests, and then Dick called Farside Base again for the status of the LST. The technicians there said the remote scope was now operating normally and laser communications with Earth also had improved.

As they started back toward the Farside Base site, about halfway down the rim ramp, Seth cried out, "What is that? I just saw a bright light flash a few hundred yards beyond the bottom of the cliff, on the farside of that small crater." They all looked to where Seth indicated but saw nothing.

Another ten yards down the ramp, Kip suddenly exclaimed, "I just saw it again. Something shiny on the other side of that small crater is catching the oblique rays of the morning sun. Let's investigate."

Dick navigated Jenny to the crater where Seth and Kip thought they saw the flash but initially saw nothing. Perhaps 100 meters in diameter, the small crater was between them and where Seth said he first sighted the flash. They drove around the crater to the other side where something shiny was sticking out of the Moon's regolith dust. Kip and Seth donned their space suit helmets and climbed out of the airlock. This was the first time either one of them had stood on the surface of the Moon and Seth found the experience exhilarating. He tried a small jump in the low gravity and rose three feet from the surface.

"Stop fooling around," Kip admonished. "Let's just go over there and find out what that object is."

A dome-shaped small object lay half-buried in the lunar soil. Seth dug around the object, extracted it, and wiped off the dust. The object proved to be a metallic sphere about the size of a soccer ball. Considering the Moon's low gravity, it was unexpectedly light and glistened in the morning sun mirroring Seth's face.

"Definitely manufactured," Seth said as he handed the object to Kip.

Kip turned it over and over in his gloved hands and commented, "This object has been sitting in the morning sun for almost an hour, yet it is still ice cold. I can feel the extreme cold through my gloves. Let's get back to Jenny where we can have a better look at it."

Back inside Jenny, all three men carefully examined the sphere taking care to wear gloves, so they did not get freezer burn. The sphere appeared to be lighter than if it had been constructed from aluminum.

"Perhaps it is light because it's hollow," Kip suggested.

Dick rapped gently on the sphere with a geologist's hammer, and the object resonated as if it was solid.

"It is definitely not hollow," Dick claimed.

The object's surface was exceptionally smooth and like a mirror reflected its surroundings. Dick examined it with a magnifying glass called a "loop" and said it was highly polished without any signs of machining or part-lines. In just a few minutes, the object had warmed up enough that they did not need gloves to handle it. Dick attempted to take the temperature of the object. In only a few minutes, it had taken on the exact temperature of the ambient air inside of Jenny.

"The object reminds me of a large ball bearing," Dick finally said.

"So, now we have two mysteries," Kip opined. "Who messed with our gyroscope power connector and hacked our computer, and who left this sphere for us to find on the backside of the Moon?"

"What makes you think it was left for us to find?" Seth asked.

"Apparently because it was only recently buried and left exposed. So, we were intended to find it," Kip said.

After they returned to the Base, Seth and Kip left the sphere in Kip's locker and immediately reported to Dr. Perkins to explain about the problems they discovered at the Annex. Seth said that someone had deliberately disrupted the Annex equipment. They did not mention about finding the sphere at the site. Peter was skeptical about Seth's claims that someone had disconnected the power to the gyroscopes and hacked the computer. Seth and Kip had no answer as to why someone could have visited the Annex and sabotaged the equipment.

After making their report to Dr. Perkins, they immediately took the sphere to the base analytical laboratory and showed it to Dr. Zach Ulbricht, a metallurgist and director from the NASA Horizon Laboratory who was visiting Farside for a meeting.

Zach turned the sphere over and over in his hands.

"Where did you find this object?" Dr. Ulbricht asked.

Kip told him that they found it at the base of the rim below the Annex.

"It's the size of a soccer ball and so light that it must be hollow," Zach assumed.

He continued to examine the sphere turning it over and over in his hands and then measured the diameter and weighed it.

"The sphere weighs about 10 ounces, appears to be metallic, smooth, and perfectly round measuring 29.68 cm in diameter with a volume of 3,268 cubic centimeters," Zach said. He placed the sphere in a tub of deionized water to measure its mass. The sphere weighted 296.8 grams when converted from the Moon's gravity to that on Earth. It floated on the water's surface displacing a minimum amount of liquid adding to Kip's suspicion that the sphere must be hollow. The density calculates to .09082 grams per cubic centimeter. Dr. Ulbricht then placed the sphere in an ultrasound machine and ran a full scan which, despite the previous presumption that it was hollow, proved that the object was solid.

"Archimedes would have been confounded by this object," Zach muttered as he again measured the amount of displaced water.

He then did an SEM scan on the surface.

Dr. Ulbricht scratched his head. "The object's surface shows no evidence of machining marks, part-lines, pitting, or roughness at any magnification. The skin is smooth down to even the molecular level."

Unable to scratch the surface for a sample, he then performed an X-ray mass spectrometer test which only added to Zach's confusion. "The main elements are platinum, indium, titanium, and rhenium. We do not possess the metallurgical means to make such an amalgam."

Finally, he performed a calorimeter test that measured the incident wavelength absorption against the emission spectrum.

"At all wavelengths, the object acts like a black-body radiator, that is, it absorbs and radiates radiation almost equally. Yet it assumes the ambient temperature. All in all, there is no known metallurgical technology which could have manufactured this sphere. I am at a loss to explain how this device should even exist. It is the most amazing and puzzling device I have ever tested. With your permission, I would like to take this object back to Earth with me next week and have it tested at the NASA Atlanta Labs."

Kip was reluctant to allow the sphere out of his control, but perhaps Dr. Ulbricht was the best person to figure out what this device was. Kip gave him permission to perform further testing at NASA.

Chapter Seven
More Trouble at the Annex

September 7

As Kip prepared to catch a ride from the USSF Horizon Moon Base back to Earth and the Santa Barbara Space Port, he received a phone call from Seth.

"Kip, if you can believe this, the remote tracking scope at the Annex has malfunctioned again," Seth said. "We would like you to return to Farside Base and take another journey with Dick and me to the LST Annex again."

The next day Kip took the shuttle back to the Farside Base and found Seth busy working in his office. After warm handshakes, Seth said that while he was glad to see Kip again, this second visit was ordered by Dr. Smithers who said the Annex scope had to be fixed as soon as possible. "This second failure of the spotter scope is as mystifying as the first was."

Kip took a seat and waited for Seth to explain.

"Last time the failure was due to a disconnected power connector, but this time it is apparent that the computer has been hacked," Seth stated. "The spotter scope is powered and performs as designed and then goes offline for a few minutes, eventually returning to normal."

"I don't think this spotter scope problem is due to hacking because I already checked and the computer remains online," Kip said. "The firewall for the LST at the Annex is impregnable, or so our computer experts claim, and the only way the scope computer can be hacked is to bypass the firewall by direct access through the computer panel at the Annex."

"Whatever the cause, without an operational spotter scope at the Annex, the LST is down again and will remain down until the spotter scope is fixed. The next dark window is next week. This afternoon we will again visit the Annex," Seth said.

Seth contacted Dick, and that afternoon the three men climbed aboard the moon buggy Jenny and proceeded across the crater floor to the Annex. Since it was now the middle of the two-week September dark period in Daedalus, they could see nothing of the craters beyond the range of their headlight beams except that the overhead stars were so brilliant that they painted the ground in a soft dim light. They arrived at the Annex four hours later, and this time they did not bring the moon buggy immediately inside the garage but parked Jenny outside. Dick remained inside Jenny as Kip and Seth donned their space suits and searched around the Annex for signs that someone had recently visited the site. Finding nothing other than their own tracks, they entered the garage, and after it was pressured, they removed their helmets. Once inside the LST spotter scope building, it didn't take Kip long to discover the cause of the LST spotter scope failure. The computer had not been hacked.

"Look at this," he said as he pointed to a petcock that delivered LN (liquid nitrogen) to the cryogenic computer module. "The petcock from the LN thermos has been turned partially off, thus depriving the computer module from receiving the liquid nitrogen it needed to operate properly."

The quantum computer used at the Annex was a cube only 6 cm on a side and must be kept at a cryogenic temperature. Because the LN supply had been partially shut off, the computer module didn't maintain a working temperature and was inoperative.

"This tampering is just like when the power connector disconnected," Kip said. "Someone deliberately tampered with the LN supply." After Kip allowed the LN to lower the module temperature to 300 degrees centigrade below zero, he tested the quantum computer to assure himself that it was now working properly. Then they installed hidden video cameras throughout the Annex and locked up and returned to where they parked their moon buggy. Before they climbed aboard, they again searched the ground for any sign that someone had visited. Other than their own footprints and the tracks left by the moon buggy on their previous visit, there was no sign that anyone else visited the Annex.

Back inside the moon buggy, Seth shared his confusion with Dick. "How can this tampering be done with no evidence of a visitor? Tampering with the power cord and the LN petcock was done by someone with the intention to temporarily disrupt the LST operation at Farside Base. Who would want to do this, and how could they do it without leaving some evidence? If they wanted to do permanent damage at the Annex, they could have done so. The tampering is more like the work of a mischievous poltergeist than a dedicated saboteur."

"I suggest that we should move some distance away from the Annex and remain here for a few hours to keep close eyes on the Annex," Dick suggested.

They agreed to spend the next several hours at the Annex and wait until late tomorrow to return to Farside. The moon buggy was well equipped for an extended stay. The four passenger seats could be inclined to a more comfortable position, and there was even a small kitchen where they could heat up and prepare meals. The bubble top of the buggy afforded a clear 180-degree view of the sky above Daedalus. Earthlight bathed the crater in a soft blue-white glow, and the lights from Farside Base lit up several square miles surrounding the base. They talked for a while and Dick and Kip began to doze off. Seth continued to survey the sky, challenging himself to name the visible constellations. This was a bit of a challenge because so many stars were visible that the familiar asterisms were difficult to identify. As he was counting stars in the Pleiades, he paused.

"I can now count thirteen stars where a minute ago I counted only twelve," he thought. Then he noticed that one star was moving from north to south across the cluster. It grew brighter as it traversed the Seven Sisters until it outshone all but the third magnitude stars in that asterism. He nudged Kip and said, "Take a look at the Pleiades. How many stars can you count?"

"Thirteen," Kip responded after a few seconds.

"Did you notice that one of them is moving?"

"Yes, I did, and it is getting brighter," Kip said.

"There has been some NASA talk about positioning a GPS global satellite system to circle the Moon, and I wonder if this is could be it?" Seth said.

Dick who had also been watching the star as it moved said, "I don't think that the GPS global satellite has progressed beyond the talking phase. It could be the Chinese relay satellite."

They continued to watch as the star moved north to south and grew brighter until it outshone all the Pleiades stars.

"I think it is moving toward us," Seth finally said. And indeed, it continued to brighten and move closer until a disk became visible. Then it stopped and hovered a thousand feet above the Annex.

"Kip, flash your laser light on the object," Dick suggested.

"It might not be wise to make them aware of us," Kip said.

"Oh, I'm sure they're aware of us. See if you can signal them," Seth said.

Kip flashed his laser directly on the object and turned it on and off several times. There was no response from the disk.

"Well, now they certainly know that we are here," Seth said.

The craft moved even closer to the Annex and then stopped about 100 meters above it. The disk was featureless and appeared to be about fifty feet in diameter. It hovered there for another couple of minutes, and then shot straight up into the star-studded sky and disappeared in two seconds.

"Wow," Dick said. "What in the world was that?"

"Something not of this world," Kip said.

"An alien UFO?" Dick asked

"I think this most assuredly is what some folks call an unidentified flying object," Seth said.

"What do you think it was?" Dick asked

"I don't know," Kip answered. "That damn thing just zoomed away with an acceleration that would have squashed its passengers, assuming there were any. Neither NASA or ESA or the Chinese has anything capable of such performance."

"So, perhaps now we now we can guess who the poltergeist might be," Dick quipped.

"Yes, but this visit tells us nothing about what their purpose might be," Kip added.

"What were they doing hovering above the Annex for two minutes?" Seth pondered. "Dick, please call the Base and ask if anything about the spotter scope positioning system has changed."

Dick called the Base and Jim said, "No, nothing that I can see. The system is preforming just as designed."

Seth turned to Dick. "Has anything changed in the transceiver shack?"

"No, nothing," Dick said. "How about our surveillance cameras," he asked. "Do they show anything?"

"No, nothing at all," Seth said.

"Perhaps we scared them off," Dick said.

"If so, they will return," Kip surmised. "Their purpose has been to delay telescope calibration and shake down tests but not to destroy it."

"Should we report this sighting?" Kip asked.

"To answer your question Kip, now we are compelled to report what we just saw."

The next day they returned to the Farside Base and Seth made his report over videophone to Dr. Ron Smithers, Project Farside director at NASA in Santa Barbara. He reported that the Annex spotter telescope had again been deliberately disabled. This time a petcock supplying LN to the cryogenic computer had been turned down disrupting liquid nitrogen to the computer module. He also told Ron about the UFO sighting that he, Dick, and Kip witnessed and that he thought there must be a connection between the UFO sightings and the sabotage.

"So... do you really think that aliens may be responsible?"

"I do," Seth responded. "There is no doubt that the damage done to the spotter scope was deliberate sabotage designed to delay the LST from beginning its scheduled research. No humans have access or could have accessed the Annex, so what else could I conclude."

"There is one piece of possible evidence," Seth concluded and then told Ron about the sphere they found and showed him a picture of it.

"So, you think that the aliens left the sphere for us to find?"

"I do," Seth said.

"Thank you for your report and honest assessment of the situation," Ron said. "I am most interested in an evaluation of the sphere. Please keep me informed."

Seth next visited Dr. Perkins in his office who knew that the spotter scope had been fixed but asked if there was evidence left by the saboteurs, and if so, did Seth have any theories about who could be responsible. Seth said like the sabotage to the power connector, this time someone tampered with the LN valve to reduce flow. This was deliberate.

"It was an act of intentional sabotage," Seth claimed.

He showed Peter a 3D picture of the sphere.

"We found this object at the base of the Annex cliff."

"It looks like a big ball bearing. What is it?" Peter asked.

"I have no idea, but Kip is analyzing it in our lab."

"Interesting, but you have no proof that this object is from aliens."

With that Peter dismissed Seth.

Seth went to the observatory and told Pam about the mysterious sphere and where they found it.

"Where is the sphere right now?" she asked.

"Kip is examining it in the analytical lab," he explained.

"May I see it?" Pam asked.

Seth took her to the lab where Kip and the Farside geologists were measuring it. Pam asked if she could pick it up and Kip said she could.

"It is amazingly light and smooth to my touch," she said. "Do you have any idea what it is?"

"Not yet," Kip said.

Seth returned to his office and Sally said that Dr. Perkins had called and wanted to see him again in his office.

As before, when Seth entered Dr. Perkins' office, he was motioned to take a seat in front of the desk. Dr. Perkins stared at Seth for several seconds before he spoke.

"I just spoke with Dr. Smithers. He told me about your report as soon as you returned from the Annex. I am disturbed not only about the content of the report, but why you called him before you reported to me. I am also concerned that you made this second trip to the Annex without my authorization."

Seth sat back in his chair and said, "The order for Kip and me to immediately return to the Annex came directly from Dr. Smithers, so the report of our findings went directly to him. I did leave word to you that Kip, Dick, and I were returning to the Annex. I have prepared a written report to you which is probably on your desk."

"I am the director of this Farside Base, and all such orders should come from this office. Your visit to the Annex without my knowledge was a breach of operational rules."

"Your concern about protocol is unfounded because the visit was directly authorized by Dr. Smithers," Seth said. "I was directly ordered by him to make this visit. I suggest you take your complaint about protocol up with him."

Dr. Perkins glared at Seth but said nothing for a few seconds. "We will continue this discussion after I read your report. Dr. Smithers says that you claim that the Annex damage was sabotage perpetrated by aliens… an unsubstantiated and ridiculous conclusion."

"First of all, my report is not unsubstantiated, nor are my conclusions ridiculous. My report has been corroborated by Kip Wheeler and Dick Puente who were with me at the Annex and witnessed the damage done to the scope and watched as a spacecraft hovered over the Annex. They also agree with my conclusion that the damage done to the pointer scope was deliberate and designed to delay our program to begin LST observations."

"If your conclusion is true, why would aliens want to delay our research?"

"I cannot answer that," Seth admitted. "All I can tell you is that the disruption to the scope was not accidental but done with deliberate purpose, yet not designed to damage the scope beyond repair but to delay the LST start of operations. Our moon buggies had not been outside Farside before Kip, Dick, and I made the recent repair visits. There was no evidence that any human other than us has been at the Annex. Perhaps the alien objectives will become clear when we begin our observation program."

"When will that begin?" Dr. Perkins asked.

Seth smiled. "Barring further delays, the shakedown of the LST could be finished next week, and our observational program can then begin."

"And what is the latest information on the sphere?" Dr. Perkins wanted to know.

"Unfortunately, there is not much to report yet on that object," Seth said. "Despite all our high-resolution analytical instruments, Dr. Ulbricht who is visiting from the Horizon metallurgical lab was unable to explain this device. All he can say is that no known metallurgy on Earth could have produced it. He has asked to take it with him when he returns to Earth next week and have it analyzed in the Atlanta NASA metrological lab."

"Keep me informed," Dr. Perkins said and dismissed him.

Seth called the members of his staff together for an impromptu meeting. Everyone was incredulous about the alien craft that Dick, Seth, and Kip had witnessed and especially about Seth's conclusion that aliens may be responsible for the sabotage of the Annex.

"Kip, Dick, and Seth were three credible witnesses who have seen this UFO at the Annex," Pam commented. "We must respect their report."

Bruce Elderly spoke up. "Stories about UFO sightings near the space stations and the Moon have circulated for 100 years, but no one has ever produced definitive evidence to confirm these sightings."

"Until now," Seth said. He opened a bowling ball bag and removed the sphere. "We found this on the crater floor near the Annex." He handed it to Jim and asked him to pass it around.

"Dr. Ulbricht has examined it and can only say that we don't have the technology to have manufactured it."

Even allowing that the sphere was real, concluding that aliens had left it and sabotaged the Annex was hard for all to swallow.

"Why would aliens want to sabotage the LST?" Pamela Hernandez asked.

"Perhaps there is something that the LST might discover that they don't want us to know about," Seth proffered.

"Could the Chinese with the Chang'e Farside Moon Project have done this?" Dr. Tammera asked.

"No," Seth said. "We found no evidence that anyone other than us had visited the Annex. There were no tracks, footprints, or anything inside that would lead to such a conclusion."

"I think the sphere is a red herring left by the saboteurs to distract us," Jim offered.

Seth concluded the meeting and found Kip in the metrological lab.

Kip told Seth that he would have to return to Horizon tomorrow and then travel to California, but he would first make a full written report to Dr. Smithers and Dr. Perkins. That report would include his opinion that aliens may be responsible for the sabotage at the Annex. They said goodbye and Seth returned to his office.

Chapter Eight
Dark Matter and the Einstein Observatory

Seth's weekly staff meeting took place as usual, with Dr. Bess Martin, Dr. Pam Hernandez, Dr. Bruce Elderly, Dr. Tess Tammara, Pete Fulmer, and Jim Karnowski in attendance. He invited Dr. Martha Benedict to this meeting to give an update on the Einstein Gravitational Wave Observatory.

Seth introduced her and then Martha smiled and stood up.

"I know that you folks are anxious to hear about Dark Matter and what the EGWO has thus far learned. Let me begin by reiterating facts that you already probably know that will help lay the foundation of my Dark Matter theory and explain what the observatory has found to support this theory. For decades physicists have unsuccessfully attempted to identify what constitutes Dark Matter. Normal matter atoms are formed with neutrons and protons each constructed from groups of three up and down quarks and electrons. DM is electrically neutral and therefore does not interact with electromagnetic radiation, so unfortunately to this day Dark Matter remains dark.

Dark Matter particles have mass, hence gravity, and their gravitational attraction on normal matter and photons is the only way that we can study it. We know that the total mass of Dark Matter in the universe is six times that of visible matter, and theoretically DM can interact with itself yet the gravity waves so generated are so faint that none of the existing instruments are sensitive enough to capture them. The EGWO is 10,000 times more sensitive than LIGO or the newer gravitational telescopes and was designed to record extremely weak gravitational waves. I believe that the enhanced sensitivity of EGWO has allowed us to detect these minute gravitational waves created by the interaction of DM with itself. This has opened a whole new window of astronomy and has allowed us to identify a candidate for DM."

Martha paused for a minute to allow that news to sink in and then continued.

"Baryons are formed by various combinations of quarks that combine in groups of three to form matter. Quarks are fundamental particles with six types called flavors named up and down, charm and strange, and top and bottom. Two up quarks and one down quark combine to form a proton, while two down quarks and one up quark form a neutron. These combinations are held together by gluons. Quarks also have properties called mass, charge, and color.

Dark Matter and visible matter neutrons and protons obtain mass when they interact with the Higgs field. Since DM atoms have no charge, they are impervious to and do not emit photons, yet gravity causes these atoms to interact with normal matter and weakly clump together to form huge clouds that surround most galaxies. Various theories have been suggested to explain what constitutes Dark Matter. One is called weakly interacting massive particles (WIMPs), and another is massive compact halo objects (MACHOs), but thus far neither of these particles have been detected. Another suspect is neutrinos, but they can only account for a small part of the DM mass. Some very massive but elusive particle is needed to explain how Dark Matter can make up 85% of the mass of the universe, and searching for this elusive particle was the subject of my research.

Dark Matter could be formed by other combinations of quark properties, flavors, and colors not limited to the top and down quarks that form normal matter. My theory is DM was formed in vast quantities along with normal matter in the big bang, and it is likely that various quark properties other than up and down combined to form Dark Matter. The six flavors of quarks along with their antiquark siblings can combine in various combinations of three quarks that carry charge and color. A proton with a charge of 1 consists of two up quarks each with a charge of 2/3 and one down quark with a charge of -1/3. A neutron with a charge of 0 consists of two down quarks each with a charge of -1/3 and one up quark with a charge of 2/3. The other flavors, strange and charm, can also combine with top and bottom quarks, but most atoms thus formed are unstable with short lifetimes. One exception is a lambda particle that is a stable combination of an up quark, one down quark, and one strange or charm quark. Other baryons such as Sigma, Xi, and Omega particles have also been identified in atom smasher detectors, but most are unstable with extremely short lifetimes that do not allow them to form stable baryons or fermions. Rarely a lambda particle forms with other protons and neutrons inside an atomic nucleus, and because the lambda particle carries a strong nuclear force, it will cause the nucleus to shrink thus betraying its presence. If some stable combination of quarks and antiquarks exists that has no net charge and a large rest mass, then they could be the source of invisible Dark Matter. Such particles would have formed in the big bang in quantities that vastly outnumbered visible mater. For instance, if a particle consisting of two heavy quarks with a -2/3 charge combines with a heavy quark that carries a +2/3 charge, it would produce a heavy atomic nucleus with a net zero charge that cannot attract an electron or a positron. A nucleus that forms from these 'odd' combinations of quarks may gather in clouds of ionic plasma that constitutes the source of Dark Matter. Matter formed from these theoretical baryons would have mass but no charge. Clumping is the process of atoms gathering in clouds where density gradually increases. Hydrogen gas will clump due to the electrical attraction of the proton in its nucleus. As the density increases, gravity accelerates the density until stars and galaxies form. Without a charge, DM cannot attract an electron and thus cannot form atoms. These chargeless particles only weakly interact through gravity, and thus DM remains in huge nebulous clouds of ionic gas, yet one with many times the mass of the galaxy it surrounds."

Martha paused for a moment to sip a glass of water and then continued.

"Two massive galaxy clusters known as Abell 2384 slammed into one another hundreds of millions of years ago. This collision was not just between two galaxies but between two clusters of galaxies. It was the most energetic event in the universe other than the big bang. The collision turned the clusters inside out thereby giving us a clue to galaxy contents and the Dark Matter that surrounds each. Galaxies are so far apart that they did about what you would expect after the collision: nothing much. The galaxies are so small compared to the volume of the cluster; they simply flew past each other like a swarm of bees. X-rays expose the fate of the hot plasma between the galaxies.

Gravity caused the gas to get all tangled up at the midpoint of the collision creating complicated bow shocks and gravitational waves. The EGWO detected these waves and helped us understand which particles made them. Dark Matter has many times the mass of visible matter, and in this collision, DM created a unique signature of gravity waves. Until the EGWO these waves were too faint to be detected, yet now our observatory has revealed them, and from this data we now have insight as to what DM may be."

Dr. Elderly asked, "So what quark combination does your study indicate that constitutes a DM nucleus?"

"We know that a DM nucleus is more massive than normal matter and has no charge," Martha said. "The triplet of quarks that constitute DM particles will be very massive and sum to a charge of zero. Neutrons have 2 down +1 up quarks with a mass of 11.6MeV/c2 and a charge of 0. The stable lambda particle has an up + down + strange quark with a mass of 102.9MeV/c2 and a charge of 0. The lambda particle has ten times as much mass as a neutron, and a similar heavy particle would be the best candidate to explain the mass we have measured in the Able cluster."

"The results from analyzing gravitational waves captured by EGWO give us a wealth of information. We suspect that the DM particles may consist of a charm + 2 bottom quarks with a mass of 7.35GeV/c2 and charge of 0. That is 700 times as massive as a neutron. There are other heavy particle candidates as well that might make up a stable DM nucleus; we have not been able to confirm the stability of these odd quark combinations yet, but we need to look for them in the residues of our collider experiments."

Seth thanked Martha for her presentation and then continued with his staff meeting.

The welcomed news from Pam was that research with the was that research with the Lemaitre telescope was proceeding on schedule.

Chapter Nine
LST Online

After years of design and construction, the LST team had recovered from the disappointment of postponing operation in August and now were anticipating calibration in September. This event was a few days away, and the renewed excitement at Farside and back on Earth was palpable. Construction of a new powerful telescope on the backside of the Moon had renewed public interest and government support for astronomy that had languished for years. Over the years whenever a new powerful telescope came online, mysteries were solved and gaps in our knowledge were filled in. Some of the most fundamental questions in science remained in the late 2100s, like the enigma of Dark Matter and Dark Energy and if we are alone. Designed to gather light from the deep universe but not specifically expected to help solve the Dark issues, no one knew exactly what we would learn with the LST but were hopeful new data would help. Without further interruptions from "poltergeists," the LST team was ready for calibration by mid-September 2067. After calibration was completed, they could begin the main mission to image and survey planets in the local star systems in October.

For almost 100 years NASA's goal has been to discover life beyond Earth. The ingredients and conditions to promote life are ubiquitous, that is, liquid water, organic molecules, and a source of energy. In the first decades of 2000, NASA deployed several missions to search for life in our own solar system, including six robots deployed on the surface of Mars, a mission to Europa, another to Saturn's moons Titan and Enceladus, and a third to Neptune's moon, Triton. But no convincing evidence of extraterrestrial life ever turned up. NASA's search for life then refocused on planets orbiting other star systems. From data gathered from TESS, it appears that most star systems harbor orbiting planets and, in several relatively close-by systems, possessed rocky planets that orbited in the so-called Goldilocks Zone, the zone around a star within which a planetary surface can support liquid water, provided there is enough atmospheric pressure to contain it. The discovery of oxygen in the atmosphere of some of these planets would indicate that life in some must exist. The light from host stars could overwhelm light from exoplanets, yet the LST could remove it. Our atmosphere filtered the spectral light from exoplanets, but the LST was designed and constructed on the airless moon to overcome these problems and to directly image and gather data from potentially life-harboring exoplanets. By late 2067 the LST team had imaged four of the TESS Earth-like planets and gathered their spectra. One planet was about the size of Earth and exhibited signs of methane in its atmospheres, an indicator that life could be present. This exoplanet also had carbon dioxide and 13% oxygen, a definitive sign of life that excited scientists.

Using his discretionary time as LST director, in November, Seth reserved time on the LST for his pet project to gather data on Janus. One mission of the LST was to explore exoplanets in the so-called Goldilocks Zone where liquid water and hence life could be possible, so combined with the other missions, Seth had limited time on the scope to study Janus. Almost 1,000 AUs from the Sun, Janus was unresolvable with existing telescopes and data could not be gathered. The LST should be able to image Janus, so Seth anxiously awaited his scope time.

Seth's mentor astronomer Michael Brown began the search for Planet Nine in 2014. Scientists knew that Planet Nine must exist due to the gravitational disturbances it had on the orbits of other objects in the Kuiper Belt. The missing planet would be large, as massive as Uranus, and would exist at the very fringe of our solar system, perhaps hundreds of AUs away from the Sun. Computer simulations gathered from the orbits of several Kuiper Belt objects predicted the planet would have a mass ten times that of Earth, slightly smaller than Neptune. It would occupy an elongated elliptical orbit with more than a forty-degree inclination to the ecliptic. Astronomers in 2014 surmised that the planet may be near its aphelion or furthest orbital distance from the Sun and at this distance would be extremely faint and difficult to detect against the plethora of background stars. As Mike Brown often said, "There is an unimaginable amount of sky out there to search." However, computer calculations had narrowed the search to a patch of sky in the Hercules constellation. At 1,000 AUs Planet Nine would take ten thousand years or longer to reach its perihelion of 200 AU where it could more easily be resolved. Astronomers are very patient, but centuries would be much too long to wait to confirm such an important discovery. Thus Dr. Mike Brown and his team patiently searched for this missing planet using the Subaru Telescope until Mike retired in 2024. It wasn't until four years later that Dr. Freedman, Seth, and the KBARP team using the Giant Magellan Telescope finally succeeded capturing Planet Nine, a faint 23.5 magnitude "star" that moved ever so slowly against a plethora of background stars.

Now, thirty-nine years since the Janus' discovery in 2028, limited by our atmosphere and the resolving power of existing telescopes, astronomers had not learned much about it. Dedicated to his goal to study Janus in depth, Seth knew that the LST on the backside of the Moon was the tool he needed to study Janus. As the LST director, Seth received discretionary time on the scope, and he and his staff used this limited time on the LST to resolve a blurry dime-sized image of Janus and study it at various wavelengths. The data they collected showed that Janus had a diameter of 13,435 miles and a thick atmosphere composed of methane, nitrogen, and carbon dioxide. Janus was indeed massive, about twelve times the mass of Earth but smaller than the radius of Neptune. It was warmer than expected with an average surface temperature of 270 degrees Fahrenheit below zero with a rocky core about the size of Earth covered by an outer ocean of liquid water. Three moons orbited Janus, one the size of Mercury. The big surprise was that, unlike some other solar system planets and moons that sustained water oceans, at this distance Janus received no warmth from the Sun, and without another planet to revolve about and provide gravitational energy, what was the source of energy that could melt water? Only two possibilities existed: the latent heat from water as it transitioned to ice or internal heat left over from the initial formation of Janus.

Another mystery was how such a large object could exist so far away from the Sun. It could not have formed out there without enough material to form a large planet. It must have formed in a material-rich region along with Neptune and Uranus and then migrated out to its present location. There was not enough material left over to build another gas giant like Jupiter, Saturn, Uranus, or Neptune, so Janus would be smaller than these gas giants. Neither could astronomers explain the elongated elliptical orbit of Janus, forty-three degrees off the ecliptic. Seth suggested an alternate theory that Janus did not originally belong to our solar system, but was an interloper, an alien planet that our Sun captured from a passing star system billions of years ago. This theory would explain the objects' eccentric orbit, inclination to the ecliptic, mass, and size. Other astronomers did not give Seth's theory much credibility because he had only conjecture and no data to back up this idea. "Perhaps more time and study of Janus can eventually answer this question," Seth said to his critics. Nevertheless, further observations with the LST were bound to help.

Chapter Ten
The Watchers

Two months had elapsed since the LST became operational, and the amount of data collected on exosolar planets and Janus filled a library of computer memory storage. Seth was in the LST control room when his cell phone rang with an urgent text from his wife. Their sixteen-year-old son William was in a San Francisco hospital with a severe infection. His prognosis was not good. Terry asked Seth to return home as soon as possible. Seth visited Dr. Perkins to inform him about his personal emergency and suggested that in his absence Dr. Pamela Hernandez would manage the LST operations. Dr. Perkins approved Dr. Hernandez as temporary manager of the LST and wished for William's speedy recovery and for a quick return of Seth to Farside.

As Seth left Dr. Perkins' office, he muttered to himself, "The old man must be mellowing. This is the first time he has treated me like a colleague and neither derisive nor condescending."

Seth held a staff meeting that afternoon to tell his team that a personal emergency back home required him to take a leave of absence. With Dr. Perkins' permission, he appointed Dr. Hernandez to manage the LST team in his absence.

Fortunately, a supply shuttle from the NASA Horizon Base was due to return to the nearside of the Moon tomorrow, and Seth could take that shuttle back to the base and then arrange transport to California. Three days later Terry met him at the San Jose Maglev station. They then drove to the University of California Hospital in San Francisco. Along the way Terry explained that Will had collapsed at the Stanford Student Union building four days ago and was admitted to the hospital. The doctors diagnosed that he had contracted viral spinal meningitis and had administered antiviral serum developed forty years ago to treat this virus. After two days in a coma, Terry said that William awoke yesterday. When Seth entered Will's room, he was sitting up and immediately smiled and said, "Hi Dad." They hugged and spoke for a few minutes. Will explained that he had no idea what had happened to him. One minute he was talking with some friends when he suddenly became dizzy and fainted. Next thing he knew was he was waking up in the UCSF hospital. Will wanted to know all about Seth's first months at Farside. Keeping their visit short, Seth told him about first light and his imaging of Janus. Seth and Terry then visited Will's doctor who assured them that Will had responded well to treatment and he should make a full recovery and be able to return to classes in two weeks. Much relieved, Seth returned with Terry to their home in Palo Alto.

A message from Dr. Hernandez was waiting on his e-mail account. She said that the LST was down again and unable to hold its position. There appeared to be another problem with the spotter scope at the Annex. Dick Puente and a technician had attempted to visit the Annex but were unable to service the scope. She didn't explain what prevented this, but she contacted Dr. Ron Smithers who agreed that both Seth and Kip should return to Farside as soon as possible to fix the spotter scope. Seth contacted Kip who lived in nearby Atherton and asked him to meet him here at his home that evening. Terry met Kip at the door and led him into the library. Seth warmly greeted Kip and then got right to the point. "We have another problem at the Farside Annex," he said as he poured a drink from a bottle of twenty-year-old Scotch. "Dr. Smithers has asked us to return to Farside."

This was unwelcome news for Kip who was preparing to travel to Hawaii where he had schedule time on the Subaru Telescope. "You know how hard it is to get time on any large telescope nowadays," Kip complained, "and I have been trying to get time on this telescope for months. A trip to Farside will disrupt my plans and I may not get another opportunity on a large scope for months if ever."

"I have discretionary time on the LST that I can share with you," Seth offered. "I'm sure the LST would be more than adequate for your exoplanet project." Kip smiled and said, "You bet it would."

"We need to have a serious discussion about alien interference at the Farside Annex," Seth suggested. "This latest Annex disruption may be another case of sabotage, but we won't know this until we arrive back at the Annex."

"I guess it is necessary for us to make another trip," Kip said reluctantly.

Seth detailed their previous trips to the Annex.

"The first time you and I visited the Annex, we found the disruption was a disconnected power connector to the gyroscopes. An easy fix and in a few minutes the spotter scope came back online. Then on the second repair visit, we discovered that the LN supply petcock to the cryogenic computer had been turned off. Neither of these disruptions could have been accidental. Somebody caused this sabotage, yet no one had access to the Annex nor was it possible that any human could have had access, certainly not the Chinese who have had a rover on the farside of the Moon since 2019. They landed astronauts there in 2028 and built a permanent base in the Von Karman Crater in 2056 and do have a moon buggy on hand. There have been no signs that the Annex site has been visited, no footprints or moon buggy tracks outside and no signs inside of a visitor. It strikes me that the sabotage was intended as a delaying tactic yet designed to be nondestructive. Had the saboteur wanted to destroy our equipment, they could have easily done so. Then on our second visit after we fixed the LN supply, we remained at the Annex to see if anyone showed up. That night we watched as an alien saucer appeared and hovered above the Annex."

"That saucer was certainly not of this Earth," Kip said. "Why do you think those aliens would have been motivated to delay the LST first light and twice disrupt our calibration process and observation plans?"

Seth frowned. "We know that no visitor from Earth has the means to access to the Annex. Neither the Russians nor Chinese are motivated to cause this problem. This leaves the aliens as the prime suspects."

"And yet when we saw the UFO that time, they did not further disrupt the spotter scope. They just made their presence known and then left," Kip said.

"I have also often wondered about the purpose of the sphere," Seth said. "I think the aliens left it near the Annex so that we would find it."

"Perhaps it was intended to be a calling card?" Kip suggested.

"A calling card... an interesting idea," Seth mused. "The aliens certainly knew that we would analyze the sphere and would be forced to conclude that its origin was extraterrestrial. I checked with the NASA metallurgical lab in New Jersey last week, and they don't have a clue as to what the function of the sphere is, what purpose it fulfills, or anything about its interior. They have been unable to extract detailed samples from its surface or penetrate the interior except with nondestructive instruments. They are befuddled and admit that no lab on Earth is better equipped to examine the sphere than they are and that no manufacturing process on Earth could have produced this object."

"If we claim that aliens are sabotaging our Farside operations, few NASA managers will accept such a conclusion as credible," Kip said.

"But we have the sphere," Seth argued. "Proof positive of an alien presence."

Kip sat quietly for a moment. "The next logical question is what's the alien's purpose in sabotaging the LST? What could they gain by delaying our research?"

"Perhaps there is something they don't want us to find out," Seth conjectured.

"Like what?" Kip said.

Seth refilled their glasses.

"Well, one of the objectives of the LST is to gather data from a few of the exoplanets that orbit in the habitual zone of neighboring stars. Several exoplanets in the habitable zone are reported to have oxygen and methane, signs of life. Perhaps the aliens are afraid that we will discover something that they don't want us to know about them, knowledge that could pose a threat to them, perhaps like discovering their home planet."

"Possibly," Kip answered. "But I don't see how such knowledge could pose a real threat to them. The closest exoplanet is 4.3 light-years away. Our present technology would take centuries to arrive at the closest exoplanet systems. We cannot pose a real threat to them."

Seth argued, "Yes, but the fact is that the aliens are here, and you and I saw them and so did Dick. This means that they must have the technology to make such intrasellar voyages practical. If we develop such a technology, we could eventually become a threat."

"Not in the near future, so why are they here now?" Kip pondered.

Seth pondered that last point for a few minutes. "I think the aliens have been observing us for centuries and want to keep their presence hidden. An example is what our anthropologists have done to study emerging peoples. Natives call them the 'Watchers.' One of our projects years ago was to engage in observing a remote tribe in New Guinea. They surreptitiously watched and studied the natives, but they never interfered or made their own presence known. Like in *Star Trek*'s Prime Directive, any interference would affect natural evolution and invalidate the experiment. Suppose, for the sake of argument, that those New Guinea natives were developing a technology that would not only allow them to discover the home of the Watchers but allow them to build a ship that could explore the Pacific Ocean. I assume that the Watchers would do all possible short of direct interference to stop them from gaining this knowledge and technology."

"That is an interesting analogy. The aliens could be watching us," Kip quipped.

Seth paused their discussion to take a call from Dr. Smithers. After he hung up, he told Kip, "Ron has asked us to catch the Maglev train to Santa Barbara tomorrow morning and visit him at his NASA office. The next day there will be a shuttle leaving for the Horizon Base, and he wants you and me to be on it."

"Do you think we should discuss this evening's conversation with him?" Kip asked.

"Definitely," Seth said. "Ron has an open mind and will listen to our theory about who sabotaged the Annex."

The next morning Seth said goodbye to his wife and son and met Kip at the San Jose maglev station. When they arrived at NASA, they immediately went to Dr. Smithers' office. As Seth suspected, Ron was receptive to their conjecture that the aliens had sabotaged the Annex.

"This could be true," Dr. Smithers admitted. "NASA has been aware of an alien presence on Earth for fifty years, yet to this day they refuse to admit it, despite the alien sphere that they now have as evidence."

"If they know the aliens are here, why would they want to keep this knowledge secret?"

"I can only guess about a reason," Dr. Smithers said. "Perhaps they fear that such an admission of aliens who have a technology much more advanced than ours would diminish the importance of NASA in the minds of those who fund it."

They said goodbye to Dr. Smithers who wished them well on their trip back to Farside.

Two days later Kip and Seth were back at Farside Base and visited Dr. Perkins' office.

"Welcome back to Farside," Peter said. "Dr. Byrne, I am pleased that your son is recovering from his illness, and Kip, it is good to see you again. Dr. Smithers called about your visit, and he trusts that the both of you can make your way to the Annex as soon as possible. The damage to our spotter scope has halted our LST research. I sent Dick Puente and a technician to fix the spotter scope last week, but they were unable to get to the Annex. On the way their moon buggy developed a technical problem and they had to return to the base. The LST has been down now for over a week."

They assured him that they would immediately contact Dick Puente and arrange for a moon buggy trip to the Annex.

"I have to wonder about Dr. Perkins' friendly demeanor," Kip said as they left his office. "He seemed genuinely glad to see us."

"Perhaps he is mellowing," Seth said with a grin.

"Like fine wine," Kip joked.

Seth met with his staff and guests Dr. Kip Wheeler and Dr. Francis Tammara that afternoon. They discussed the problem with the Annex that had again shut down the LST. Seth explained that he and Kip would be visiting the Annex tomorrow and he suspected sabotage was the cause of the disruption.

"Who would have the ability to sabotage our equipment three times and what would their motive be?" Dr. Vince Germain asked.

"I do not know," Seth admitted.

"Perhaps the Chinese who have had a presence on this side of the Moon for decades," Dr. Pamela Hernandez conjectured.

"Yes… but unlikely," Seth said. "Their rovers and the Shenzhou series of moon landings have all been geological expeditions limited to the Aitkin Basin and inside of the Von Karman Crater. Why would they want to sabotage our LST project? We even have one of their astronomers, Dr. Chang Chow, on our LST staff. Chang is a member of the CNSA (China National Space Agency) and the last person I would suspect of collaborating with saboteurs."

Dr. Tammera spoke up., "Rumor has it that you and Kip think aliens are responsible for this sabotage. Dick Puente also says that you have actually seen an alien spaceship at the Annex."

"This is true," Seth admitted. "Kip, Dick, and I saw a spaceship hovering over the Annex. We also found the sphere near the Annex, an object that even our best metrological scientists cannot explain. We think the aliens left it there for us to discover. Kip calls it a calling card."

This admission caused quite a stir among Seth's staff members, some of whom found the alien theory hard to accept.

"It is hard for us to swallow the assertion that NASA knows about alien presence and have kept this information hidden for decades," astronomer Bruce Elderly said.

"Well, we can only guess at their reasons, yet it is what it is, and we did see a UFO at the Annex," Kip said.

Seth said that tomorrow he, Kip, and Dick Puente would visit the Annex. Then he dismissed his staff and returned to his office.

Early the next morning, Kip, Seth, and Dick, along with electronics technician Paul Morrisey, climbed into the moon buggy "Jenny" and headed out across the Daedalus Crater toward the Annex. They skirted the central peak and navigated toward the southern rim of the crater. As they drove beyond the central peak, about 4.8 kilometers east of the peak and 24 kilometers from the southern rim, Jenny suddenly stopped. Everything inside and outside Jenny went dark.

"We've lost power," Dick said. "The motor, outside lights, and my control panel are out."

Dick and Paul donned space suits and went outside to access the engine compartment where the batteries were located.

After a few minutes, they climbed back onboard.

"We could find nothing wrong with the batteries or the electronics module. We are dead in the water so to speak," Dick said in frustration. "The self-powered short-range transceiver appears to be functional, but Farside is not responding to our transmissions."

"The transceivers have self-tested as normal, but it appears that our outgoing signal is being blocked," Paul said.

"So, what do we do now?" Kip asked.

"I suggest we should just stay put," Seth said. "We have three days of supplies on board, and when Farside does not hear from us by this evening, they will come looking for Jenny in another moon buggy."

Dick had an important thought. "We can assume that the repair crew buggy will experience the same failure as Jenny; if so, we will have two dead moon buggies. We should don our space suits and walk back to where we last had communications and warn the rescue buggy to meet us far from Jenny."

They walked two miles away and three hours later, Nora showed up to take them back to the base. Nora remained fully operational, so the mechanics hiked over to Jenny to examine Jenny's electrical system. They found nothing wrong and returned to Nora. After ten miles on the way back to base, Jenny suddenly indicated that she had come back to life. The entire electrical system was now operating normally.

"What in the world is going on here?" Kip asked.

"I find it interesting that Jenny was affected a short distance from the peak and apparently two miles away Nora was not," Dick said. "It is as if an RF field affected Jenny."

"It could be a field emanating from the central peak to inhibit our power system," Paul conjectured.

"It is as if someone did not want us to get to the Annex," Kip added.

They then drove back to Jenny and Kip and Paul piloted it back to base.

After they returned to home base, the Farside mechanics went to Jenny and gave it a thorough checkup. They couldn't find anything that would explain the sudden loss of power.

Kip, Dick, and Seth then met again with Dr. Perkins in his office.

"Seth, I'm beginning to believe in this alien theory of yours," Dr. Perkins admitted. "However, we must get the Annex spotter scope back online. I think you should give it another go."

Seth agreed and the following day Seth, Paul, Dick, and Kip again headed toward the Annex this time with two moon buggies, Jenny and Nora. Jenny's twin sister Nora with two technicians and a mechanic on board followed Jenny about two miles back. Dick took Jenny's route as before, and again at the same distance from the central peak, Jenny lost power, but Nora who was about two miles behind didn't. Jenny's transmitters as before were unable to get a signal out to the base.

"Nora must wait in place to see if Jenny again powers up," Dick said. "Farside has only two operational moon buggies, and even though Nora is not affected at this distance, if Nora approaches Jenny, she may also lose power. If so, we all will have a forty-kilometer walk back to the base. I think it is best to wait and see if Jenny again goes back online."

Dick was correct, for after waiting an hour inside Jenny, the power came back on and long-distance transmitters were again able to transmit. Dick contacted Farside and reported their status. Jim and Paul then walked the two miles over to Jenny and checked her out. All was normal so they piloted her to Nora.

Both Nora and Jenny then returned to base. Once back, Seth, Dick, and Kip again met with Dr. Perkins.

"It is apparent that we are being prevented from making a repair trip to the Annex," Seth said. "Jenny lost power and may do so again. We don't want to risk another outage. I suggest that we get one of the NASA shuttles to take us to the Annex."

"If there is some sort of power blackout field from the central peak, won't we be risking the shuttle?" Dr. Perkins asked.

"I'm thinking that the disruption emanating from the central peak is intended to disable our moon buggy but would not disable a shuttle high over the central peak."

"That is only an assumption," Dr. Perkins pointed out.

"Yes, but to get the LST back online, we must fix the spotter scope at the Annex. We have no other option," Seth argued.

"If, as you say, the blocking signal comes from the central peak, why not try again but take a route with the moon buggy that avoids that area?" Peter suggested.

"Good idea but we do not know if this is true," Seth said. "The safest and fastest way is to use the shuttle." Peter thought for a minute and then said, "A supply shuttle is due here later today and you can take it to the Annex tomorrow."

Dick said, "In the meantime, I will ask our technicians to get the third moon buggy operational just in case it is needed in the future for another rescue attempt."

Dr. Perkins then called to find out the ETA of the shuttle from the NASA Horizon Moon Base.

The supply arrived as scheduled, and the next day with Dick, Kip, Seth, and computer technician Paul Morrisey on board, they flew high over the Daedalus Crater toward the south rim.

Dick instructed the pilot, "Don't go directly to the rim, but make a wide circle and approach the Annex from the south side of the crater."

Dick explained his unusual instructions, "I suspect that there is a field emanating from the central peak that is intended to prohibit anyone from approaching the Annex from the crater floor, but I don't think they expected anyone to approach from above beyond the rim."

The shuttle flew over the edge of crater at 5,000 feet and then circled back to approach the Annex.

"Land on the flat a few hundred feet south of the Annex and we will walk to the Annex," Dick instructed the shuttle pilot.

The shuttle landed without incident. They dressed in their space suits, and Paul, Dick, Kip, and Seth walked to the Annex.

Once inside the airlock and entry room, Paul used his scanner to search for any spurious RF transmissions. He discovered a carrier transmitting at 8.42 GHz and traced its origin to a black box attached to the back of the Annex wall. It was not an alien transmitter but one of NASA's own transmitters transmitting a narrow beam signal to the central peak. Paul disabled it and announced, "That's the end to the device activating the inhibitor at the central peak."

They went inside the spotter scope room and opened the main control panel, and Paul began testing to find out what had disabled the scope. It didn't take Paul long to discover the reason that the spotter scope was not working. The main computer had been programed to run an endless self-test program that locked out normal operations. Paul ended the self-test routine and the spotter scope again returned to normal operation.

"Our firewall is impenetrable, and the self-test routine can only be activated from this control panel," Paul said. "This was a simple way to disable the computer, but it means that someone had to be physically here to do this."

Dick downloaded the security camera's memory to his handheld computer. The memory chips were all blank. "Someone erased the all the security memory," he said.

"Probably the same person or persons who disabled our computer and installed the inhibiter transmitter," Seth said.

They searched around the room for some evidence of an intruder but found nothing other than the NASA transmitter which they disabled and took with them to analyze. No fingerprints, skin cells, footprints, or any useable DNA evidence. "The place is as clean as a whistle," Dick said. They locked up the Annex and returned to the parked shuttle. Once back inside, Seth contacted Farside Base and told them that the spotter scope had been repaired and the LST team could now get back to work. As the shuttle headed back to Farside, they discussed the purpose behind this sabotage at the Annex.

"Obviously, the saboteurs do not want us to continue research with the LST," Seth said. "But why should this be so?" Paul asked

"There must be something that they are afraid we will discover with the LST," Kip supposed.

Seth thought for a minute and then said, "Returning to my analogy about some anthropologists called the Watchers spying on primitive New Guinea natives, suppose that those natives discovered the Watchers' observation post and found some of their tools and observed their ship come and go. With their cover now blown, the anthropologists would realize they were adversely affecting the natural development of these indigenous people and they would have to abandon their experiment and make a strategic withdrawal. The natives now curious who the Watchers were wanted to learn more about those people and the tools that the scientists unwittingly left behind. Eventually using what they had found and learned, the natives began to construct a seaworthy ship that would allow them to explore their island and search for the home of the Watchers. The last thing the scientists wanted was for the natives to learn about and be influenced by any advanced technology. In every case where an advanced civilization interacted with native peoples, those people suffered destruction and a collapse of their society. I have to wonder if the aliens fear the same thing will happen to mankind should we learn too much about them and their technology."

"You're saying that mankind is some alien anthropologist's experiment that could go wrong, one that has been ongoing for decades?" Dick said.

"Aliens may view us as an emerging technological society that should be observed," Kip conjectured.

"Kip could be right. To the aliens we are an exotic experiment that needs to be watched," Seth said.

"If that is true, I suppose those alien watchers would do all possible not to have their cover blown yet inhibit us from gaining their technological knowledge, and the LST is a tool that will help us learn about other worlds and possibly even discover their home," Kip said.

Seth pondered that idea. "One thing I have never been able to wrap my head around is the distance any aliens would have to travel to visit Earth. The closest star to the Sun is Alpha Proxima in the Alpha Centauri system. It is over four light-years distant, and even if the aliens possessed a technology that would allow their spaceships to achieve some fraction of the speed of light, it would take over a century to make a round trip from the nearest star system. Such a journey would be impractical."

"Unless they have a technology that does not limit their ships to the speed of light," Dick added.

"There is no technology that is not subject to Einsteinium physics," Kip argued.

"Folks have been reporting seeing 'flying saucers' on Earth for years," Seth added.

"Well, the three of us saw one their vehicles at the Annex, so we know they are visiting here right now," Dick said. "Perhaps their life span is hundreds of years rather than decades so that a long journey is not impractical for them."

"And then again they left us the sphere which remains a mystery," Kip added.

They sat quietly for the rest of the return trip to Farside pondering all this.

When the shuttle landed, Dick, Seth, and Kip went directly to Dr. Perkins' office and reported what they had learned at the Annex.

The director listened carefully to the report and then replied. "So, you claim that a computer self-test program was activated at the Annex, and this was evidence of sabotage caused by aliens?"

"Yes, that is exactly what I am claiming" Seth said.

"Could the computer have imitated the self-test program through some Trojan virus or remote hacking?"

"No," Kip replied. "Not according to Paul Morrisey. Paul said that the self-test program could only be initiated from the main computer control panel. The self-test program is buried deep inside menus that would require the physical presence of someone to initiate this program. No Trojan virus or hacker could do this."

"I guess then we're back to square one: the 'aliens did it' theory," Peter said sarcastically.

Seth was offended. "It's more than a theory—there are no other plausible explanations."

Dr. Perkins frowned, "Seth, I still cannot believe that the saboteurs are aliens. What proof do you have that the aliens are the only people who could have done this damage? Could someone like the Chinese Chang'e folks who have a helium-3 mining operation on this side of the Moon have sabotaged the Annex?"

"Yes, while it is possible, it is improbable. It is true that the Chinese are mining helium-3 in Anticum Basin which is hundreds of miles away, but there is no evidence that they visited the Annex," Seth responded. "When all possibilities have been eliminated, then the simplest explanation should be considered. The aliens are here and all three of us have seen their spaceship at the Annex."

"Claiming to have seen a flying saucer is not proof," Peter said. "Thousands of people have claimed to see flying saucers, but no one has ever presented substantial physical evidence."

"How about the sphere that we found," Kip reminded Dr. Perkins. "That is physical proof of an alien presence."

Dr. Perkins sighed. "Oh yes, the sphere. What about it?"

Kip responded, "I recently spoke with Dr. Zach Ulbricht at the NASA Horizon Base metrological lab who has put the device through every analytical test known to modern metrology without a hint as to what its purpose is or from what it is made. It is impervious to anything but a nonphysical probe. Other than radiological probes and physical measurements, the only conclusion he can state is that no metallurgical process on Earth could have manufactured this orb. Zach sent the sphere to NASA's main metrological lab in Atlanta who confirmed his findings or lack thereof. The lab director, Dr. Tsing, now has the sphere. I also spoke with him and he said his lab could learn nothing from further testing. He agrees with Dr. Ulbricht that the sphere was not manufactured on Earth."

"Yes, but NASA says that there is no proof that aliens made it," Peter said.

"I guess the only proof that could convince NASA would be if an alien spaceship landed at NASA Headquarters and the pilot asked to be taken to the leader," Kip mocked.

Dr. Perkins changed the subject. "Now that Paul has fixed the computer at the Annex, what is to prevent someone from returning to the Annex and damaging the scope again?"

"We should be thinking about a way to prevent this," Dick suggested.

"Like what do you suggest?" Peter asked.

"Like having full-time guards stationed at the Annex," Dick suggested.

"That is an excellent idea. Let's do it," Peter said.

"The Annex was designed to have a small overnight facility including some bunk beds and a kitchen," Dick said. "We should ask for a couple of guards to be there 24/7."

Dr. Perkins agreed and said that he would have someone assigned immediately.

Jack Bickford and his wife Marylin were part of the Farside security team and volunteered to guard the Annex. Dick picked Jack and Marylin up and drove them to the Annex and left them with four weeks of supplies. John contacted the base each morning with a surveillance report. In the first few days, they checked the security cameras daily but had nothing to report. Nor were there any further disruptions of the Annex equipment.

Chapter Eleven
Revelations

Now that the LST was back online and fully calibrated, normal astronomical research could proceed as scheduled. Time on this instrument was precious, and many of those nations and astronomical societies who helped finance the Farside Base vied for time on the instrument. Because the farside of the Moon was in direct sunlight for two weeks at a time, observation time was limited to the two weeks of darkness each month.

As director of the LST, Seth had 10% of available scope time to pursue his own project, which was to gather more data on Janus. Because of all the interruptions caused by the sabotage at the Annex, Seth had yet to exercise his discretionary time. Keeping his promise to Kip, he shared his time so that Kip could continue his work with the Kuiper Belt Astronomical Research Project known as KBARP. Now that his time on the telescope had arrived, he sat down in the LST control room and programed in the coordinate of Janus. The picture of an astronomer peering into the eyepiece at the end of a long tube was history. Today astronomers sat in a comfortable desk chair and peered at a high-resolution screen as they sent commands to the telescope via their computer.

This was the first time since his observation time in Hawaii that Seth had the opportunity to observe Janus, and now with the high resolution and clarity of the LST, he was able to see Janus as never before. He established that the surface was covered by water ice and nitrogen ice frozen at a frigid 320 degrees centigrade below zero. When he tried to measure the diameter with more precision, he noticed that the limb of Janus seemed asymmetrical, with a noticeable bulge on one side. Upon his next observation a few days later, a moon emerged from the limb of Janus. As the moon fully emerged, he studied it in detail. It was about the size of mercury, and its surface of water ice and carbon dioxide ice was 160 degrees centigrade warmer than that on the surface of Janus. The moon's distance from Janus was

240,000 miles with a rotational period of two weeks. Because of the strong gravitational force from Janus that distorted and heated the moon, there was a strong possibility of a liquid water ocean beneath the moon's surface. After more observations, Seth located two additional small moons much further away from the planet, each smaller than Sedna. The IAU did not find the news of a large moon circling Janus all that surprising. All the outer planets had several moons, and there was every reason to believe Janus would also have some. The IAU named the large moon Zwicky after the twentieth-century physicist. Out here in deep space where the Sun was only a bright star, the surface temperature of Zwicky was expected to be 300 degrees below zero, but the warm surface temperature indicated that the gravitational force of the host planet, the latent heat of freezing, or some other process made it possible for Zwicky to harbor a liquid ocean beneath the surface.

In the meantime, Kip continued to make observations for his research project KBARP while the rest of Pamela's LST astronomy team searched for rocky exoplanets and large exomoons inside of the habitual zone of various star systems.

At one of Seth's weekly staff meetings with Kip as a guest, Pamela reported that five systems had been discovered harboring Earth-like planets or moons. One system LST3590 looked particularly interesting.

"This sun was a red dwarf about 1/2 the diameter of our Sun and 12 light-years away. Six rocky planets orbited LST3590, three of which had atmospheres and were in the so-called Goldilocks Zone where liquid surface water could exist. LST3590B, the planet closest to the Sun, was three times the size of Earth and tidally locked to its sun. The second planet, LST3590 C, was 2.25 times the diameter of Earth. Unfortunately, none of these exoplanets showed signs of oxygen or methane, but there are dozens and dozens of other candidates we have yet to explore."

"I'm still having a hard time understanding how the aliens could have made this voyage here," Kip admitted. "Assuming that these aliens are technologically a thousand years ahead of us and have a means that would allow them to travel at up to 1/2 the speed of light, it would still take decades or centuries to make such a trip. Such a trip is not practical."

"Yet, we know they are here on Earth and Moon despite our inability to explain it," Seth said.

"I do not understand why the aliens are so intent on preventing us from discovering their home planet and yet left the sphere as a calling card," Bruce Elderly commented.

"Perhaps they are worried that if we can identify their home, we might someday want to make a voyage there," Jim Karnowski suggested. "Up to this point, their crafts have been observed, yet the centrifugal motions of these objects indicate that they are pilotless drones. There have been rumors of crashes, and even if true, they have kept us from learning very much about them. The sphere seems to be a violation of their prime directive."

"We are not a threat to them, at least not for now," Kip said. "It will be decades, perhaps centuries, before we have developed a technology that would make such a trip practical."

Seth interjected, "Yet our technology is growing by leaps and bounds, and perhaps that growth concerns them. It was only 100 years between the first flight at Kitty Hawk and our landing on the Moon. Now just 100 years later, we have explored all the planets including Pluto and established permanent bases on the Moon and Mars. In another 100 years, who knows what we will achieve."

"We are all aware of the universal speed limit imposed by the speed of light, but it would take an inconceivable amount of energy to achieve any large percentage of that limit. It is more likely that they have a technology not yet imagined by humans," Bruce offered.

Everyone agreed with that bit of logic.

Seth concluded the meeting saying, "aliens are here, and somehow, they made the trip."

Chapter Twelve
A Visitor from Interstellar Space

G len Arnold and Helen Luray, NASA geologists who had arrived at Project Farside in August, had not yet had a chance to explore the Daedalus Crater. They asked Dick Puente if they could accompany him and Seth on the monthly shuttle visit to the Annex to resupply the caretakers Jack and Mary Bickford. Now that the disrupter had been destroyed, Dick agreed, and they left Farside Base on a Monday morning in mid-October.

Helen asked Dick if he could circle North around the central peak so they could investigate a large boulder that stood out on satellite pictures of the Daedalus Crater. She said that the strange shape and dark color of the object demanded a close-up investigation. About the size and shape of a school bus, the boulder differed from all the thousands of other boulders and rocks scattered about the crater floor. A few astronomers argued that the boulder was an asteroid, yet it lacked any evidence of an impact crater or the skid marks that it should have made when it plowed into the Moon. Other geologists presumed that the boulder was ejecta from an ancient volcano, but Helen said only a close inspection could end the argument.

Dick was happy to comply with their request and easily found the boulder in question about 4.8 kilometers north of the central peak. They could find no evidence of surface marks on the Moon that would have indicated its arrival. Seth, Helen, and Glen donned space suits and exited the shuttle to investigate the boulder. Immediately it became apparent that this object was an asteroid and not volcano ejecta. The shiny black object was pockmarked with small craters indicating that it had been in space for a long time. They took pictures and measured the length as 9.2 meters, a girth of 3.4 meters, and height of 3.6 meters. They determined with their spectrum analyzer that the asteroid was composed of mostly iron and nickel, but other heavy metals were also abundant. They broke off several samples to analyze back in the base metrology lab and returned to shuttle. After the visit to the Annex, they returned to the Farside Base and Glen and Helen took the samples to the metrology lab for analysis. They confirmed that the object was a most unusual iron-nickel asteroid. A detailed metallurgical analysis proved that it was unlike any other asteroid known to science. Iron or element Fe 26 has many isotopes. The ratio of one isotope of radioactive Iron (Fe 60) to nickel (Ni 60) indicates the age of a sample. Fe 60 has a half-life of 2.6 million years, and the ratio of Fe 60 to Ni 60 confirmed that this asteroid was older than the age of our own solar system. It is an ancient visitor from another system at least 800,000 years older than our own 4.4-billion-year-old solar system. The entire sample was slightly radioactive and contained 76 % iron, 14% nickel, and 7% of iridium. There were also 3% of other heavy metals including titanium, rhodium, and thorium. The measurements of the boulder indicated a total volume of 113 cubic meters. From their analysis and measurements, the density was 12.8 g/cubic centimeter or 12,800 Kg/cubic meter, considerably higher than the 7.65 g/cubic centimeter for iron. This added up to a mass of over 1 million kilograms. A big asteroid indeed, so they named it Goliath. Another mystery is why it lay on the surface without any signs of an impact crater or skid marks that should have marked the massive asteroid's collision with the Moon. It looked as if Goliath had gently landed on the Moon, only disturbing a few top centimeters of moon regolith. Glen decided to send samples of Goliath to Dr. Zach Ulbricht from the USSF metrology lab in New Jersey for confirmation and further analysis. Coincidently, Dr. Ulbricht was presently visiting the metrology lab at the Horizon Moon Base.

Two days after their return from the Annex, Dick Puente and Seth visited the Farside metrology lab to find out what Glen and Helen had learned about the unusual asteroid. They shared the data they had gleaned from the asteroid samples. Seth was impressed with the amount of data that the geologists had gathered, and he realized that the percentage of elements would be immensely helpful in identifying which ancient exosolar systems might have the right mix of heavy metals to evolve habitable worlds. Most amazing was the asteroid's age. Helen said the evidence confirmed by the data indicated that this asteroid did not originate in our solar system. The composition of our asteroids tells us much about our solar system and the composition of the original cloud from which it condensed. That cloud originated from a third generation of supernova's, where all materials on the periodic table were formed. The materials in Goliath indicate that it was formed in an older distant solar system that condensed from a second-generation cloud not as rich in heavy metals.

Dick offered a theory about how Goliath may have arrived on the Moon.

"Obviously, this visiting asteroid landed gently on the Moon's surface. Perhaps when asteroid arrived from outer space after the formation of our solar system, the Moon captured it and for a time it orbited our Moon. Influenced by the Moon's gravity, eventually it spiraled toward the surface matching the Moon's speed and softly landed on the backside without making much of an impact."

"And there is another mystery to consider," Dick added. "I think that the Annex was hacked to delay the LST because the aliens do not want us to investigate exoplanetary systems."

Pam added, "The LST project has already discovered six solar systems where Earth-sized planets orbit in the so-called Goldilocks Zone where liquid water can exist. Goliath can help us determine which of these systems contain the same mix of materials and may be the home of our alien visitors."

At Seth's weekly staff meeting with guests Kip, Dick, and Helen in attendance, Pam reported that armed with the metrological data from Goliath, her team began to gather the spectroscopy of each extraplanetary system's star. One star's spectroscopy, 2MAS J2308298-045622, a red dwarf sun about 1/3 of the mass of our Sun and 22 light-years distant, was an exact copy of the mix of materials in Goliath. Six planets orbited this system which they named Corinth, two of which were in the Goldilocks Zone. The two inner planets were tidally locked to the sun, and the three outer planets were outside the "Goldilocks" Zone. However, the remaining planet about 1.25 the mass of Earth had an atmosphere of nitrogen, water vapor, CO_2, 16% oxygen, and .04% of methane.

"Definite signs of life," Pam said. "I believe that life is ubiquitous throughout the universe and intelligent life may exist in our sector of the Milky Way. As evidenced by the ancient age of the meteor Goliath, the Corinth system from which that object came is 800,000 years older than our solar system. This is enough time for life to have evolved on an Earth-like planet in that system. If life evolved into intelligent beings, then this civilization could be thousands of years older than our human civilization and technologically very advanced."

"I have always had trouble accepting that aliens could make the many light-years travel to Earth," Seth said. "Nevertheless, if these alien civilizations are thousands of years older than humans, they may have technology beyond our imagination and could make a twenty-two light-year journey practical. I believe that these aliens have been visiting Earth for hundreds, perhaps thousands, of years and remain wary about revealing themselves or their home to us. Credible UFO reports have been posted for dozens of years. Buzz Aldrin on the Apollo 11 mission reported that a large cigar-shaped object was following them between Earth and the Moon. Other astronauts have made similar claims. I believe that aliens find us scientifically interesting, and when in the last 100 years our technology advanced to allow space travel, they became increasingly alarmed that we would discover their home and went so far as to disrupt the Lemaitre telescope project."

Helen reported that Dr. Zach Ulbricht from the USSF metrology lab was skeptical of the data she and Glen obtained from the Goliath boulder and asked for additional details be sent to the USSF Metrological Laboratory in New Jersey for confirmation. Dr. Ulbricht argued that the Goliath samples were taken from samples extracted from the surface of the asteroid. After millions of years in space, cosmic rays may have altered that asteroid's surface materials. He suggested obtaining some core samples.

Two days later, Dick and his team prepared the moon buggy named Jenny for the trip to Goliath. Tricia Gomez, the Farside Base nurse, said that she had not been outside of the Base and asked if she could go along. Pam also asked to join them. Seth agreed and he and Tricia, Glen, Helen, technician Paul Morrisey, Dr. Pamela Hernandez, and Kip boarded moon buggy Jenny piloted by Dick Puente. Dick drove Jenny out onto the Daedalus Crater and headed toward the central peak thirty kilometers away. Now ten days into the two-week daylight cycle on the backside, the Sun was at forty-five degrees and cast a long shadow from the peak and from the many large rocks scattered about the surface of Daedalus. Goliath lay about five kilometers north of the central peak. When they were about three kilometers away from the central peak, Jenny suddenly went dead. All power to Jenny's drive motors and control panel ceased. They tried to raise someone at Farside Base, but no one responded.

"This is just like our previous experience when on the way to the Annex Jenny died a few kilometers north of the central peak and all communications were lost," Dick said. "I thought we destroyed the transmitter we found at the Annex."

"We did, but they must have placed another one to activate the inhibitor on the central peak," Kip surmised. "The RF field around the central peak that disabled our moon buggy before is not only keeping us from the Annex but also from Goliath."

"We should do as we did last time Jenny got stuck and walk some distance away to see if we can reestablish communication," Seth suggested. Kip and Paul suited up and walked a kilometer back and attempted to contact Farside Base. Fortunately, the short-range person-to-person communications continued to work, but there was no response to Paul's attempts to contact the Base. After walking another kilometer west, they still couldn't contact anyone at the Farside Base.

Paul suggested, "I think this 'dead zone' may extend even further away from the central peak than we thought. Let's walk five more kilometers west of the central peak and continue to try to raise Farside."

When Dick heard that Kip and Paul were walking even further than planned, he announced that it may be a while before they returned. Helen then asked Dick how far they were from Goliath. He said Goliath was four kilometers north of their present position.

She suggested, "While we are waiting for Paul and Kip to return, Glen and I should take the drill and walk to Goliath to obtain some core samples." Glen agreed and Seth offered to join them. It took them ninety minutes to walk to the asteroid, and once there they drilled four core samples from each side and then returned to Jenny. Expecting that after three hours by now Paul and Kip should have returned, Seth grew worried when they hadn't returned and contacted Paul. "We are on the way back," Paul said. Two more hours elapsed before Kip and Paul finally returned to Jenny.

"We were unable to raise Farside Base even though we walked eight kilometers west of the central peak," Paul reported. "But not to worry. When we have not returned to the Base as planned, the Farside folks will realize that we must have had a problem and will come looking for us in the rescue moon buggy."

Glen did not look reassured. "Won't the same interference that has caused Jenny to die also cause the rescue moon buggy to die?"

Seth agreed with Glen that it might. "The rescue moon buggy will follow our tracks toward the central peak. We all need to suit up, walk several kilometers following our own tracks, and wait to meet the rescue party."

Pamela was pensive. "What if it takes the folks at Farside Base some time to organize a rescue? Do we have enough liquid oxygen (LOX) and water in our individual tanks to make the long walk and wait for the rescue buggy?" she asked.

"There is a rescue party ready if we need help. We have plenty of oxygen, enough for two days," Dick assured Pamela.

"The aliens obviously do not want us to study Goliath and its origin," Dick claimed. "They are trying to keep us away."

Helen smiled. "Well, unknown to the aliens we already have the core samples."

They all suited up and walked three kilometers away from Jenny. Paul tried several more times to contact the Base, but still no one answered his calls. Seth said that they should walk another three kilometers toward Farside and make themselves as comfortable as possible as they wait for the rescue moon buggy. Twelve hours later when the rescue moon buggy had not appeared, Dick and Seth began to wonder what was taking them so long. Then Dick and Paul decided to walk a few more kilometers further away and try again to contact the Base.

"Seth, wait here fifteen minutes and then have the team follow us," Dick suggested.

As they walked, Paul shared his thoughts with Dick. "I believe the 'dead zone' is an area where all electrical activity is being interfered with. The zone appears to be centered on the central peak and extends within a radius of at least five or six kilometers. Enter that zone and electrical devices and communications are disrupted. I think the aliens placed a transmitter on the central peak. Once we are beyond this zone, then everything should return to normal."

Finally, three kilometers further away, Paul finally raised the Base and told them of their situation. He handed the transceiver to Dick.

"Is another buggy on its way to rescue us?" Dick asked Greg Partridge, his chief mechanic who he had left in charge of the rescue team.

"Not yet. We are having trouble with both of the other moon buggies," Greg reported.

Dick was confounded that Greg and the rescue team had waited so long to prepare the other moon buggy Nora for a rescue. Anger began to boil up inside of him.

"The whole team exited from the safety of Jenny, and now that we cannot depend on a timely rescue, we will have to begin walking toward Farside. We have limited supply of LOX. How long do you think it will be before Nora or the other moon buggy will be on the way to rescue us?"

"We are not sure, but I will contact you as soon as I have an answer," Greg said.

"We will have the team begin to walk home, and once we are all beyond the dead zone, Seth or I will contact you hourly," Dick said.

"Not very encouraging, was he?" Paul said.

"No, he wasn't. I cannot understand why Greg waited for our rescue call to prepare Nora. It really makes me angry."

When the entire team joined them, Dick explained that he had contacted Farside, but rescue was not imminent.

"We have a limited supply of LOX, so we should assume that rescue is not imminent and begin walking back to the Base," Seth said.

"That is over thirty kilometers away," Tricia exclaimed.

"Yes, but we can do this," Seth reassured her. "It should take us less than sixteen hours to walk home. We cannot wait for the rescue team, so let's get going."

They formed a single file and Seth took the leader position with Dick in last place to make sure that no one lagged behind. They stopped every hour to rest and take a drink of water as Seth again contacted Farside and reported their position. After six hours of trudging through the megalith, first Tricia and then Glen slowed their pace. Dick asked them if they were ok. Tricia said that she was winded, and Glen complained that his legs hurt. Dick asked Seth to stop. "We are still eighteen kilometers away from Farside Base," Seth said, "and we cannot depend on the rescue vehicle meeting us part way home. We will rest for a while and then we must trudge on."

Kip reported that his oxygen tank gauge now read that he only had five hours of LOX remaining. Seth asked everyone else to check their LOX supply. Everyone reported that they had sixteen or more hours of oxygen remaining. Dick checked Kip's tank for a leak but found none.

"I think Kip's tank was never completely filled," Dick said while growing angrier about the team's inept preparations supervised by Greg.

"Well, we have at least ten hours of walking remaining," Seth said. "We will have to transfer LOX from one of our tanks to Kip."

"There is a fundamental problem with that plan," Paul said. "The LOX tanks have not been designed to fill one tank from another, and we do not have a means to interconnect tanks. We cannot share LOX with Kip."

Seth called Farside, reported the critical LOX problem, and asked for an update about preparing the rescue moon buggy. Greg answered that they still had not figured how to fix either of the moon buggies and it would be at least until tomorrow before they launch either one of them. Seth knew that Kip's LOX supply would run out long before that. Dick asked to talk with Greg.

"Have you figured out what the problem is with Nora?" Dick asked.

"The air pump that pressurizes Nora's cabin is intermittent and we don't have a spare," Greg said.

"Take the pump from the other moon buggy and install it in Nora," Dick ordered.

Greg paused for a few seconds and then replied, "We thought of that, but the two pumps are incompatible."

"Well then improvise. If you can't get Nora working and out here to rescue us in less than five hours, Kip will run out of oxygen."

Seth told the team about Greg's bad news.

"If we start walking right now at a fast pace and do not stop to rest, we may cut the ten hours to five," Paul suggested.

"No, Kip will use even more oxygen on a forced march," Tricia insisted. "We must find an immediate solution to Kip's LOX problem."

Dick asked, "Does anyone have an idea how we might improvise a connection from one of our tanks to Kip's tank?"

Helen and Glen searched their backpacks. Both carried a few items that any geologist would always have with them. "We have a few miscellaneous hardware parts," Glen said.

Dick said that he carried the emergency toolbox from the moon buggy. Tricia said that she had a complete first aid box that included a three-foot-long piece of medical tubing with connectors intended for transfusions, but the connectors were incompatible with the LOX tank hardware. With the various hardware from Glen's backpack and tools in his toolbox, Dick attempted to modify the tube to transfer LOX from Seth's tank to Kip's. After three hours of feverish work, Dick had the transfer tube in hand. He connected his tank and transferred half of his own LOX supply to Kip. None too soon because Kip only had just an hour and forty-five minutes of oxygen remaining when the transfer began. With that emergency averted, the team began the remainder of the trek home to the Farside Base. Ten hours later, they were safely inside the Farside Base. Glen and Helen immediately took the Goliath core samples to the metrology lab for analysis. Helen sent the results and samples by shuttle to Dr. Zach Ulbricht at the Horizon USSF metrology lab. Since the core samples were never subjected to cosmic rays over the eons of time, they were less radioactive than previous samples, but other than that fact, the age analysis was the same as obtained from the previous surface samples.

Two days later Kip received an urgent call from Dr. Zach Ulbricht who updated the results of his lab tests. Kip thought it would be about the Goliath core samples, but it was not.

"The NASA Atlanta folks have confirmed that the tests I performed at the Moon Base on the sphere were correct. However, they report that the diameter is now 28.32cm, 1.36cm less than what I measured it just one month ago. The sphere appears to be shrinking, yet the mass is the same 296.8 grams as I originally measured. Only the density has increased!"

"What does this mean?" Kip asked.

"It means that if the sphere continues to shrink at this rate and still retain its original mass, in six months the sphere will be the size of a tennis ball with density greater than any known material on Earth."

"Will it shrink out of existence?" Kip asked.

"I do not think so. At some point the atoms will resist coming closer together. We have only conjecture to describe what will happen as the sphere continues to shrink. I have to wonder what the aliens had in mind by leaving this object for us to find and why it has been designed to shrink."

"Zach," Kip said, "This is astounding news. We have disparate bits and pieces of this alien presence on the Moon which includes hacking the Annex computer. What did you confirm about Goliath?"

"We confirmed the previous analysis of Goliath, but the only hard evidence of alien presence we have is the sphere. I am going to talk with Seth, Dr. Perkins, and Dr. Smithers and ask for permission to organize a teleconference of key NASA scientists to discuss what we know about these aliens."

"That is an excellent idea, and I will be looking forward to participating in this teleconference."

Chapter Thirteen
A Visit to KARMA

Peter called a staff meeting with his directors, Seth, Martha, and Francis. He announced that Dr. Jio Zhongquin, the director of the Chinese KARMA moon base, had called with a request. Project Farside had recently installed a new device on the Lemaitre telescope that greatly improved short wavelength (ultraviolet to gamma ray) data. The device was called a USWAF, for ultra-short wavelength filter and amplifier. The heart of this unique optical bench was an integrated SOS (silicon on sapphire) computer chip called TETRA. There were only two of these optical benches in existence, and Farside had both. The Chinese wanted to copy this device as they had with much of US technology but did not have access to the silicon on sapphire technology and could not copy the TETRA chip that was the heart of USWAF.

Dr. Zhongquin proposed a trade: two liters of precious He-3 for the spare USWAF optical bench. This trade was very tempting because Farside's supply of He-3 was critically low; in fact they had only a three-month supply remaining, and without He-3 the Farside fusion reactor would shut down. No power, no Farside operations. The only supply of He-3 was from the Horizon Moon Base mining facilities on the nearside, and they advised that they will be unable to provide additional quantities for another four months. Two liters of He-3 would be enough to power Farside for a year. Jio also proposed if Farside would deliver the optical bench by their moon buggies, their team would be welcomed guests and could have a tour of the KARMA base and mining facilities. For years NASA had asked the National Science Foundation of China (NSFC) and the Chinese Academy of Science (CAS) for permission to visit KARMA, but they have steadfastly refused. The Chinese built their permanent moon base and mining operation in the Von Karman Crater in 2062 and named it KARMA. The entire purpose of the KARMA science mission has remained a well-guarded secret as has details of their He-3 operation.

"This is a very good opportunity for Farside and NASA, and one we should take," Peter said.

Seth was very skeptical of the Chinese proposal. "It has been difficult to trust the Chinese NSFC. They have broken their agreements with NASA in the past. This proposal sounds sweet, but it presents two questions: First, why are they so anxious to have our optical bench? We had no idea that the NSFC even had a telescope at KARMA, nor do we know what their astronomical mission is. Second, it is unclear why the Chinese are proposing that we make this trade in person. KARMA is 700 miles away over unexplored territory. Why not make the proposed trade using NASA shuttles and not risk our team by making such a long and dangerous trip?"

"I suggested as much to Dr. Ron Smithers when I advised him of the Chinese proposal," Peter said. "He reminded me that NASA had requested this visit many times and said that the USA is desperate for He-3 and this visit is a unique opportunity to learn how we might improve our extraction process. Fifty years ago, we ran our country on fossil fuels, but now we run it on He-3 which fuels our fusion reactors that feed the electric grid. We cannot mine and process enough He-3 from the inefficient Horizon operations to satisfy the growing US need. It is vitally important for us to make this visit to KARMA, specifically to learn about the Chinese He-3 mining and processing facilities. This is an opportunity to have our eyes on the KARMA site and learn about their extraction operation."

Martha spoke up. "I am also skeptical of the Chinese intentions and their lack of transparency. They have operated a laser gravitational interferometer on the Gobi Desert for years but will not share their data with us. I suspect they may have a hidden agenda."

Francis pointed out that Seth was right—this would be a hazardous journey. "Von Karman Crater is over 700 miles away and the backside of the Moon is not at all like the front side. It is a virtual Swiss cheese of big and small craters that will make navigation difficult and risky. I'm not even sure our moon buggies can make such a hazardous and long trip."

"The importance and danger of such a journey is obvious," Peter said. "Yet it is of national importance and is what NASA and Dr.

Smithers want us to do. I am asking Seth to organize a volunteer team and form a plan to make this important visit."

Seth said he would do so and report back. He called his staff to a meeting consisting of Jim Karnowski, Bruce Elderly, Vince Germain, Dick Puente, Mark Fulmer, and Pam Hernandez to discuss this mission. After he explained Jio's KARMA phone call and Dr. Smithers' and NASA's response to the proposal, he then asked Bruce, who had extensive knowledge of the Moon's farside, to plan a route to Von Karman Crater. Bruce projected a map of the farside and expanded it to show details between Daedalus and Von Karman craters. Then he overlaid an altimeter map.

"As you can see there are many intervening craters and altitude changes between here and there. This will take me some time to plan details of the safest yet most direct route. This journey is not going to be a cake walk."

Seth offered, "I will call for a general meeting of the entire Farside team, explain the proposed mission, Bruce's proposed route, and ask for volunteers."

At that meeting, Seth explained the mission, took several questions, and asked for six volunteers. Two dozen hands went up. He took down their names and then met with his staff to select six members.

They chose astronomer Vince Germain to pilot the moon buggy Jenny, Dick Puente as mechanic, Bruce Elderly as navigator, Helen Luray as geologist, Jim Karnowski as lead astronomer and technician, and Tsing Chow as translator. Tsing worked for Dr. Jio Zhongquin at KARMA before he was assigned to Farside. His doctorate was awarded at UCLA and he knew the KARMA staff. He spoke both Mandarin and English equally well.

Seth met with the selected travel team and explained that they would be taking two moon buggies, both Jenny and Nora. Each would be outfitted for a three-week journey, but KARMA would have to resupply them for the trip back home.

"Unless there are some objections, I propose that Dick will drive Nora and Vince will drive Jenny. Helen and Jim are assigned to Nora and Bruce and Dr. Chow are assigned to Jenny."

Jim asked, "This is a long trip, and the buggies were never designed for such a journey. Are there sufficient power and supplies in the buggies for such an extensive trip?"

Dick answered, "Each buggy will carry tanks of hydrogen and oxygen adequate for three weeks, and hydrogen fuel cells will charge the batteries and combined with oxygen to provide water."

"I am asking Vince to lead this expedition," Seth said, "so I am suggesting that the team be named the Germain team." Everyone agreed.

Seth then asked Bruce who would be their navigator to show the proposed path they would take to Von Karman Crater. Bruce displayed a holographic map of the backside terrain on a 4x10 foot table. He then zeroed in on the area between Daedalus and Von Karman Craters.

"This will be a daunting and dangerous trip. I think it will take us about twelve days each way. The geology is pockmarked with tens of thousands of craters, most less than a mile or two but six are over a hundred miles wide. All these obstacles will have to be circumnavigated. The direct distance between Daedalus and Von Karman is 741 miles, but avoiding all these many craters will make for a zigzag trip of up to a thousand miles. Both Daedalus and Von Karman lie on the 179-degree backside longitude which we will generally follow south, and the latitude will be about 175 degrees west."

Bruce showed a close-up picture of Von Karman Crater. "It is about the same size as our crater but four times deeper, about 41,000 feet. It lies near the northern border of the huge south-pole crater Aitken. Fortunately, the crater Leibniz on its northern border struck millions of years after Von Karman was formed and caved in part of the northwestern wall which may provide a means for us to access the deep crater floor."

Seth thanked him and said, "Dick and Vince will supervise the mechanical preparation of the moon buggies, and they will make sure that each buggy is properly supplied. I have spoken with Dr. Zongquin at KARMA and they are anxious to host the Germain team. We will take a week to prepare, and to take full advantage of the Sun, we expect to leave on June 7, the next sunrise on the backside."

At 6am on June 7, the Germain team gathered in front of Jenny and Nora. Directors Seth, Martha, and Francis were there to wish them farewell. Peter's absence was noted by all. After handshakes and a few words of encouragement from Seth, the team climbed into Nora and Jenny, and after the airlock was evacuated, the outside door opened, and the Germain team drove out onto Daedalus Crater as the Sun peeked over the eastern rim. Nora followed Jenny as they headed south toward the southern rim forty-eight miles away. Their first challenge was to climb over the 9,800-foot-high Daedalus Crater wall. About ten miles from the rim, Vince stopped to search for a pass and found one at 5,300 feet where part of the southern rim had been breached by another impactor. Most of the wall had fallen into the crater floor thus creating a convenient ramp and forming two terraces. By noon of the first day, they were outside the crater and headed southwest toward their first goal, Aitken crater, 220 miles away.

Bruce plotted the most direct course possible, but dozens of small craters less than a mile wide had to be carefully avoided. They passed to the west of the forty-mile-wide crater Racan on the second day and despite the many diversions made good progress southward. They were alongside the 140-mile-wide Crater Aitken by the third day.

Bruce consulted his maps and said the next challenge was to find a way between the lines of adjacent craters 340 miles south of Aitken that threatened to block their path. A dozen large adjacent craters extended on an east-west line for 150 miles. "We will either have to find a way between Van de Graaff and Nassau whose crater rims are only 1500 meters apart or divert 170 miles east to avoid this line of large craters."

They arrived at the valley between Van de Graaff and Nassau on the fifth day and viewed the steep 350-foot rim walls that formed a canyon between the two adjacent craters. The canyon floor was littered with boulders and rocks, and Helen commented that these two craters must have impacted when the surface of the Moon was sill plastic, thus forming crowns around each crater and the canyon between them. Vince decided the canyon was wide enough to drive between the two crater rims, so the next day, they entered it and drove cautiously between these two huge crater walls. Ten miles into the canyon, Vince came upon a shallow depression about thirty feet in diameter and a few inches deep. He did not hesitate to begin crossing the depression, but the minute he entered, his front tractors began to sink into the soft regolith. Vince realized that it was a sinkhole and immediately tried to back out, but the font tractors sank even deeper and the back tractors couldn't extract Jenny from the sinkhole. Vince called Dick and explained their problem.

"We are stuck in a sinkhole. Cautiously approach Jenny but stay clear of the sinkhole. Move close enough so that Jack can put on a space suit and hook a cable onto Jenny so that Nora can drag us out of this depression."

Dick drove up behind Jenny as Jack put his space suit on and dragged a cable from Nora and hooked it on Jenny's back end.

"It appears that this depression is a small crater filled to the brim with loose regolith," Jack said. "The more you try to extricate Jenny, the deeper she will sink. Fortunately, your back tractors appear to still be on solid ground, but your front tractors are mired in the sinkhole. Let Nora do all the work to pull you out."

Jack stood by as Nora tugged on the cable. Slowly, foot by foot, Jenny gained a tenuous perch on the edge of the sinkhole.

"I think you can now try to back up," Jack instructed. Once Jenny was on solid ground, Jack returned to Nora, and both buggies backed up so they could navigate around the filed crater.

"That was a close one," Vince said. "Had I driven any further into the depression, we would never have been able to extricate Jenny. Even now the crater seems to be growing deeper as if the surface regolith is falling into a void hidden beneath the sinkhole. As we traverse this canyon, we will have to be vigilant and avoid crossing any more depressions."

"We have not seen anything like this crater before, Helen said. "I suggest it may be a unique result formed by these two craters as they formed so close together. Nevertheless, there could be more hidden sinkholes like this one, so caution is warranted."

Four days and two hundred miles further, they found themselves at the northern rim of the 250-mile-wide crater Leibnitz. To the south of Leibniz lay their destination, Von Karman. Bruce said they would have to navigate around the western wall of Leibniz and approach Von Karman from the north which should take two or three more days. Nine days after leaving Farside, the Germain team was standing on the northeastern rim of the Von Karman Crater looking at the crater floor forty thousand feet below.

"Oh my God, it is deeper than I ever imagined," Helen exclaimed.

"Bruce, how in the world are we going to get down there?" Jim asked.

Bruce was searching the rim and floor of the crater through his binoculars. "Jim, part of the northern wall collapsed when Leibniz impacted, and it is only 14,000 feet high. The debris from the collapsed rim will provide a means to safely navigate to the crater floor. If you look through your binoculars, you can make out KARMA located on the western side of the crater. All you can see is an igloo-shaped small building that probably is the entrance to their underground facilities and a blockhouse that must be the fusion reactor. There is also a transparent dome that must be the roof of the underground observatory."

Vince placed a call to Dr. Zongquin to tell him that they had arrived at Von Karman and planned to work their way down to the crater floor and be at KARMA in two or three more days. Jio told them to park on the pad outside of the igloo and instructed that they should put on their space suits and wait outside of their moon buggies for the igloo door to open.

The 14,000-foot descent to the floor was daunting, but using the natural ramp formed from debris and regolith, they carefully picked their way down. When they arrived at KARMA, they parked on the ramp in front of the igloo and donned their space suits as Jio had instructed. The igloo showed no sign of a door or entrance, but within a minute a hidden airlock door slid open. They entered the air lock and after the chamber pressurized, an elevator door opened. A voice told them to take off their space suits and hang them in lockers and then enter the elevator. The five-minute ride down to the KARMA facility was stomach wrenching and uncomfortable. When the elevator door finally opened, they stepped out onto a platform where Dr. Zongquin and several other managers waited to greet them. Jio shook hands with Vince and then with all the rest of the Germain team.

"It is a pleasure to meet you folks and welcome to KARMA," Dr. Zongquin said. He then introduced his staff, including his second-in-command Dr. Lao Wong; Dr. Jiang Xin, the director of the observatory; and Dr. Hui Kwok, director of the mining operations.

"I'd also like you to meet Yu Yan who will be your guide and interpreter. From now on you will be in her capable hands. Right now, we must return to our offices."

Yu had a beautiful smile and said, "I am pleased to meet each one of you folks. It is my pleasure to be your companion for the next several days." Vince complimented her on her perfect English, but she smiled and said, "I have a master's degree in communications earned at USC." Then she led them on a tour of the KARMA facilities.

Six three-story block buildings and a large Quonset hut had been constructed in a cavern much smaller than the one at Farside. Yu said that the cavern was 100 meters long, 75 meters wide, and 145 meters tall and had been excavated from solid rock. A soft yellow light illuminated the entire facility and seemed to emanate from the ceiling. The buildings surrounded a green grass-filled park filled with small flowering shrubs and miniature cherry blossom trees. Each building displayed a large alphanumeric sign starting with A-1 and ending with D-6. The Quonset hut was designated by the letter "J."

Yu began the tour by taking them into the ground floor of building A-1. Offices on three levels surrounded the hollow center of the building which held a well-appointed lounge and atrium garden complete with a fountain. Jungle plants and fern trees reached skyward from the atrium. Next, she took them into the dining hall which spilled out into the atrium and said that they should consider A-1 to be their home base. To the left of the dining hall was a conference room designated for their use. She then took them to C-3 and showed them the dormitory that would be their sleeping quarters. There was a separate room for Helen. The next stop was the Quonset hut. Inside a botanical garden filled the one-acre building with neat rows of beans, rice, vegetables, and miniature fruit trees. One side housed several tiered rows of a hydroponic garden.

"We feed all our employees with what we grow in this building," she said with obvious pride.

Their final stop for the day was the observatory. Dr. Jiang Xin greeted them at the door and led them onto a platform and elevator that took them on a ten-minute 5,000-foot ride to a chamber underneath the transparent dome. The telescope was unimpressive, a modest Cassegrain design with a 2.4-meter primary mirror, about the same size as the eighty-year-old Hubble telescope.

"We do not need a large telescope to accomplish our mission which is to explore deep space. Nevertheless, without your optical bench, we will not be unable to fully achieve our main mission," Dr. Xin explained.

"Exactly what is that mission?" Vince asked.

Dr. Xin answered, "We want to better understand the formation and evolution of the first galaxies after the big bang. Did they form with the aid of black holes, or did they form by direct collapse bypassing the black hole phase? Or perhaps by some other means presently unknown to us."

"How will our optical bench help achieve that mission?" Jim asked.

"Your device is an ultra-short wavelength filter and amplifier. At the heart of this unique optical bench is an integrated silicon on sapphire amplifier chip called TETRA. This chip allows a telescope to explore selected wavelengths from ultraviolet to gamma rays. We have nothing like this device, so we appreciate the trade negotiated for your optical bench. I assume you have brought it with you, Dr. Xin said."

"Yes, we did," Vince said. "It is still in one of our moon buggies."

Dr. Xin then took them back down and into the observatory control room. Three astronomers sat at desks looking at their high-resolution computer screens. One screen showed the telescope's magnified optical view, a second screen was an ultraviolet view, and yet another screen depicted the analysis of observed elements.

"Your optical bench will provide a new window with which to examine the elements in deep space even in the primordial so-called dark zone," Dr. Xin said.

"Will you share your data with the International Science Foundation or NASA?"

"Dr. Zongquin will have to answer that question," he said.

Yu said that it was time to return to building A-1 for dinner in the dining hall. The dinner featured five courses specially prepared for their visitors. Dr. Lao Wong joined them for dinner.

"Tomorrow, Yu will take you to visit with Dr. Kwok who will describe the mining operations," Lao said.

"We have been looking forward to touring the mine and extraction facility," Helen said. "It will be the highlight of our visit to KARMA."

The next morning, they met with Yu for breakfast, and afterward she took them to building C-3 where they met with Dr. Hui Kwok in his office. He led them into a conference room with a large table on which rested a two-meter-high scaffold, a miniature mock-up of the extraction plant. Vince assumed this mock-up was designed to help them better understand their upcoming tour of the actual extraction plant.

Dr. Wong began his presentation by detailing the function of each of the eight sections stacked on top of each other inside the scaffold.

"Raw material consisting of regolith and rock arrives from the mine by a long conveyor belt and is fed into the upper section where it is crushed into a fine powder by a series of rollers and then fed into the next section where it is mixed with water forming a slurry. The next section is the furnace where the slurry is heated to 2,250 degrees C and reduced to a magma where the various gasses including helium are vaporized, separated, and fed into several colored pipes. The next section is the chiller where the helium gas is cooled to -270 C where it becomes a superfluid liquid and is then fed into a separation tank where helium, He-3, and He-4 stratify into three distinct layers. Let me demonstrate."

A tall one-meter diameter glass cylinder and a thermos sat on the table next to the scale model. Dr. Kwok filled the glass cylinder with supercooled liquid helium from the thermos. Despite the low moon gravity, it took only ten minutes for the fluid to separate into three distinct layers. Dr. Kwok explained that the upper 95% was normal helium, the mid 5% layer consisted of 0.4% He-3, and the bottom layer with 3.6% of the total was He-4.

"Actually, we use centrifuges to separate the helium isotopes," Dr. Kwok admitted, "but this demonstrates the process of how helium isotopes are separated."

"This is then the end of my formal presentation," he said and then led them back to his office. "Are there any questions?"

Helen asked a few questions about the separation process, but the others saved their questions for the tour of the plant.

"Since you have no further questions, Lu will now take you back to A-1."

The Germain team sat there dumbfounded. "No tour?" Brad whispered to Vince.

Vince addressed Dr. Kwok. "Thank you for this demonstration and the model of the extraction process, but we were expecting to see the mine and tour the actual extraction plant rather than only see a model."

"This would be very difficult," Hui said. Tsing whispered in Vince's ear, "That translates to *not possible*."

"Dr. Kwok," Vince objected, "part of our trade agreement with Dr. Zhongquin includes a visit to the mine and to tour the extraction plant… firsthand."

Dr. Kwok smiled and explained, "We do all our mining underground with a tunnel boring machine, so there is not a mine to show you. It is dangerous for you to visit the extraction plant, so we have provided this model for your benefit."

"An actual visit is part of our agreement," Vince said.

"Too dangerous," Dr. Kwok repeated.

"What is dangerous?" Vince asked.

"There is a danger from corrosive dust," Dr. Kwok said.

"The presentation did mention a rock crushing section, which I assume would produce dust. What elements in the dust are corrosive?"

"Many elements," he said. "Bad for lungs. Therefore, I cannot take you on a tour of the extraction plant."

"You have workers at the extraction plant, do you not? If the dust is dangerous, they must wear protective gear that you could also provide for us."

"A tour of the extraction site is an essential part of Dr. Perkins' agreement with Dr. Zhongquin," Seth said.

"I suggest that you take this up with Dr. Wong," Dr. Kwok suggested.

Seeing that they were getting nowhere with Dr. Kwok, Yu Yan came to the rescue and offered to take the team back to building A-1 for lunch. When they arrived in the cafeteria, Dr. Wong joined them.

Dr. Wong tried to explain. "I understand that you wished to visit the extraction plant. This is not possible. We have shown you a complete model of this plant and invited you to ask any questions. This should be sufficient."

"It is not sufficient," Vince said emphatically. "Our agreement was to visit the mining and extraction plant, not just see a cardboard model. Unless the entire agreement can be fulfilled, we cannot complete our part of the bargain."

Dr. Wong looked offended and tried to explain. "It is too dangerous for you to visit the site; the dust is corrosive. Many elements in the dust generated by crushing the rock would be harmful to your lungs. We are responsible for your safety."

Vince was angry but tried to not show his irritation. "If you are worried about us being exposed to the dust, you can provide us with the proper protective gear. But without this promised visit, we cannot deliver the optical bench to you."

"I was told that Dr. Xin already has the optical bench," Dr. Wong said.

Dr. Xin had joined the conversation and pulled Dr. Wong aside for a moment and spoke in hushed Mandarin. Dr. Chow whispered to Vince that they were discussing the optical bench that Dr. Wong thought we had already delivered to Dr. Zhongquin, but Dr. Xin corrected this misunderstanding.

Dr. Wong asked Vince if the optical bench was still in the moon buggy.

Vince replied that indeed it was and then added, "The optical bench will remain there until the entire agreement including the extractor tour and the He-3 is delivered as promised."

Dr. Kwok and Dr. Wong excused themselves and left the hall.

Vince excused Yu and discussed this event with his team.

"Peter and NASA management was extremely specific that this was to be a trade—the optical bench for two liters of He-3 and a visit to the mining and extraction plant. We can compromise on the visit to the mine, but I will not concede on the visit to the extraction plant," Vince said.

Jim looked angry. "The Chinese are trying to pull a fast one. The dust issue is a red herring, and the cardboard model was created to satisfy their end of the bargain. They do not want us to see the actual plant and perhaps learn more about their efficient extraction process."

That afternoon Yu said that Dr. Wong spoke with Dr. Zhongquin who allowed that they could visit the extraction plant, so she took them back to Dr. Kwok's office where they donned protective gear and then boarded a transporter which took them into a shaft that extended a thousand meters beyond the main cave and opened into a large chamber. Inside was an iron scaffolding thirty meters tall and ten meters on each side. The structure held pastel-painted tanks at each of eight levels, moving belts, kilometers of color-coded pipes, and electrical cables that led everywhere.

"No pictures," Dr. Kwok warned as they stood on a platform at the top of the structure.

A gangway surrounded the outside of the scaffold and spiraled down to each level. Dr. Kwok offered to lead Vince, Jim, and Helen onto the gangway, but he asked Yu, Dick, Dr. Chow, and Bruce to remain behind. At the first level, a long belt delivered chunks of rock and regolith into a bin that fed material into a series of roller crushers. The fine powder from the last rollers emptied into level two and mixed the material with water. The slurry emptied into a blast furnace on level three and then to a second furnace on level four, where the resulting gasses were captured and separated. The helium was fed to a refrigeration unit on level six.

"The furnace heats the material and drives various gasses off including the helium which is captured and filtered in the next step of the process," Dr. Kwok explained. "It is then cooled to 270 degrees below zero where the helium becomes a liquid. He-3 and He-4 are further cooled to -273 degrees where they become a superfluid. In the final stage of the process, these isotopes are separated from helium by centrifuges, much in the same way that I demonstrated for you at my office.

Helen carefully sketched details of what she saw as they made their way down the gangway through the several levels. It was obvious to her that much of the detail had been missing from the model, but after their tour the extraction plant operation became much clearer to her.

"As you can see," Dr. Kwok said when they arrived at the bottom, "the extraction facility is just like the model I showed you except that it is much larger. If you have any questions, save them until we return to my office."

As far as the danger from dust was concerned, no cloud of dust was visible, and although all the workers wore masks, they wore no other protective gear other than orange jumpsuits. At the bottom of the facility, a refrigerated containment vessel was marked He-3 from which a worker was busily filling two one-liter ceramic thermos bottles. A second much larger vessel was marked He-4. Dr. Kwok placed the two one-liter bottles into an insulated double-wall titanium box equipped with a small portable refrigerant unit.

"Here are your two liters of He-3 as promised," Dr. Kwok said as he handed the box to Vince. They then took an elevator back to the platform where Yu and their companions patiently waited for them and they all climbed back into the transporter.

When they returned to Dr. Kwok's office, Dr. Wong was waiting for them. "I see that Dr. Kwok has given you the He-3," Dr. Wong said. "I trust that Dr. Kowalski and Dr. Jing Xin can now go out to the moon buggy and fetch the optical bench."

Vince nodded and said, "We will be glad to do so."

They were led back to the room where the model was. Helen and Jim both had some specific questions which Dr. Kwok tried to evade.

"I noted by your separation demonstration that four times as much He-4 is separated than is He-3. What is the application for He-4?" Helen asked.

"Research," Dr. Wong said.

"We understand that there are several elements and rare earth isotopes that exit the crusher. Other than helium, what other elements and isotopes do you extract?"

"Mainly iron, aluminum, calcium, magnesium, titanium, potassium, and phosphorus. Some of these elements are radioactive like phosphorus 41," Dr. Kwok said. "Hydrogen, oxygen, nitrogen, and argon gasses are separated from helium out of the first furnace."

"Why do you mine in tunnels just below the surface?" Helen asked.

"We discovered that the amount of He-3 in rocks and regolith below the surface is much higher that the regolith at the surface. This is because the Sun, whose ejections transform helium into He-3, was much more active millions of years ago."

Yu took them back to A-1 where Dr. Xin and Dr. Wong were waiting.

"Dr. Germain, Dr. Xin would now like Dr. Kowalski to accompany him to the moon buggies to fetch the optical bench," Dr. Wong said.

Jim and Dr. Xin then departed to go back to the surface and fetch the optical bench from Jenny. Jim carried the He-3 container box with him and hooked it into the refrigeration system inside Jenny. He gave the optical bench container to Dr. Xin and they both returned to A-1.

"Now that our business has been concluded," Dr. Wong said, "I trust that we have entered a new era of scientific cooperation between China and the NASA foundations. The NSFC has agreed to share the data captured with the optical bench and trust you will do likewise. It will be too dangerous for you to travel back to Farside in the dark, so please be our guests for six more days until Sunday when the Sun again rises. In the meantime, Yu Yan will continue to be your host and guide. Make yourselves comfortable at KARMA while you wait for the next sunrise." Dr. Wong and Dr. Xin then excused themselves to return to their duties. At dinner that night, Yu excused herself to take care of some personal business. This gave Helen the privacy she needed to show the team her sketches and impression of the extraction factory.

She reported that critical process steps were omitted in the model but are included in her sketches.

"This Chinese separation technology is ten times as efficient as is our factory at Horizon. I estimate that they can extract twenty liters of He-3 and sixty liters of He-4 each week. This is enough He-3 to fuel 90% of the fusion reactors on Earth. Soon, China will own the He-3 market. The good news is that I learned a lot about the details of their process that we can apply to our own Horizon extraction factory to increase our production of He-3. There was good reason for the Chinese to try to prevent us from an 'eyes-on' tour of their facility. They did not invite Bruce or Dr. Chow on the scaffold tour because they thought that Bruce had toured the Horizon extraction and mining facility and understood the basic process. They did not know that I had visited Horizon and was familiar with that operation and as a geologist I obtained a lot of insight into their process. Their mistake."

Yu joined them at Breakfast the next morning. "In the holographic theater tonight, there will be a special showing of the 2045 Olympics held in Beijing. You are all invited to attend as our special guests. Because the 2020 Olympics in China had to be cancelled due to the COVID-19 virus and due to world tensions, the Olympics was suspended and not resumed until 2045 when China again hosted the event. We have a holographic presentation of that Olympics."

"We will be pleased to attend," Vince said.

That night the Germain team met in the theater along with other invited guests including the KARMA management staff. Those in attendance sat in seats arranged a horseshoe circle in the center of the room. The lights dimmed and the presentation began. Holographic theater movies where the images appeared on a stage in front of the audience had been the movie theater staple in the USA since mid-century, but the imagery they were now treated to was like nothing Vince and his companions had ever seen. They were surrounded by the 3D image as if they had been transported to the actual location. The sights and sounds of the Beijing Olympic stadium encircled them. The images seemed real and not just a holographic illusion. In the center of the stadium, the 500-meter track competition was in full swing, with the Chinese team in the lead. The crowd let out a defining roar as that team crossed the finish line taking first and second places. The movie continued for another ninety minutes covering several events and concluded with a tour of the Forbidden Palace. The Germain team was impressed with this cinematic technology that the USA had not yet achieved.

On Friday Jim Karnowski asked Yu to see if he could visit the observatory again to observe how they were doing with the optical bench. Yu did so and reported back that Dr. Xin claimed, "this would be very difficult."

"Another one of those polite Chinese 'No' answers," Dr. Chow said.

Two days before they were scheduled to return, Dr. Jiang Xin sent a message through Yu that he would like Jim to meet him in the observatory. Jim thought this a strange request since he had been previously denied a visit but went to the observatory as requested.

He met with Dr. Xin who said that they were having trouble with the optical bench and asked if Jim could help. Jim agreed to have a look, and when he examined the installation, it was clear that the bench had not been properly collimated. It was an exacting process that Dr. Xin's staff did not know how to do. He showed their technician how to perform the proper alignment and then Yu returned with him to A-1. The next day Jiang called to thank him and said that the instrument was now performing as they had hoped.

Sunday arrived, and the Germain team prepared to return home. Yu took them to the elevator platform where Doctors Zhongquin, Xin, Kwok, and Wong waited to say goodbye. They had not seen Dr. Zhongquin since they first arrived. The Chinese wished the team a safe journey and said that they appreciated this visit from Farside. Vince thanked them for their hospitality and invited a KARMA team to visit Farside Base. Dr. Zhongquin promised that they would do so if the Farside shuttle could pick his team up. With special thanks to Yu, they all shook hands. The Germain team entered the elevator and returned to the surface.

After donning their space suits, they exited the igloo and climbed aboard Jenny and Nora. Once everyone was seated, Vince turned Jenny on and checked the instrument panel. He noticed a yellow light that indicated the status of the hydrogen fuel cells.

"This is not good," Vince said. "Something is wrong with one of our fuel cells. Bruce, will you get your helmet back on, and then go outside and open the battery panel and check to see if the fuel cells are ok?" When Bruce returned, he said that someone had disconnected one of the cells and removed it. When later on it was reinserted, the power cable had not been properly connected while the moonbuggies were being reprovisioned.

Vince was flummoxed. "So, someone removed a fuel cell from Jenny and then returned it?"

"Yes," Bruce said. "That is apparently what happened. The yellow warning light went out after I made a better connection. While we were being hosted at KARMA awaiting the return of sunlight, the Chinese came out here and removed a fuel cell so they could copy it."

"Now we know why the Chinese were so intent that we deliver the optical bench by way of our moon buggies," Vince groused. "They wanted to get their hands on one of our innovative hydrogen fuel cells to understand our efficient design so as to improve their own cells."

"How unethical," Dr. Chow said. "It makes me ashamed of my own countrymen."

"And they weren't even smart enough to make sure they left no evidence," Bruce said.

"When we get back home, I will report to Ron Smithers and he will have to file a complaint with NCSF," Vince fumed.

The Sun had not yet risen over the eastern ridge of Von Karman when they started for home, so they followed their old tracks and climbed to the ridge of the crater where the Sun now shone. Bruce plotted a route identical to the one they had traveled on from Daedalus to Von Karman. The two-week journey back to Farside was uneventful, and when back home they handed the precious box of liquid He-3 to Dr. Jensen who managed the fusion reactor. The team met with the Farside directors the next day for a debriefing. Dr. Perkins then asked Helen to go to Horizon as soon as possible and meet with the He-3 mining and extraction managers to relay the information she had gathered at KARMA.

She said she would catch the next shuttle.

Chapter Fourteen
The Teleconference

As Dr. Kip Wheeler promised, he organized a video teleconference of NASA scientists involved with alien research. Participants were folks with Project Farside, the NASA Atlanta metrology lab, the Horizon Moon Base, SETI, and NASA operations throughout the USA. Some scientists included in this April 21, 2068, teleconference were Seth Byrne; Ron Smithers, LST astronomer; Peter Perkins, Farside director; Zach Ulbricht, director of the Horizon metrology lab; Pamela Hernandez, LST principal astronomer; Helen Luray, Farside geologist; Francis Tammera, director of the PW Radio Telescope; and Dr. Eric Cobb, SETI director and a longtime advocate for alien presence on Earth.

Dr. Kip Wheeler introduced the principal participants and then stated the primary objective of this teleconference.

"For much of the twentieth century and early this century, folks throughout the world have reported seeing unidentified flying objects. Many of these sightings were verified yet defied rational explanations. Many believe that the UFOs are crafts manufactured here on Earth, while others think they have an extraterrestrial origin. During the first two decades of this century, the number of reported sightings peaked, and then by the late 2020s mysteriously all but disappeared until very recently. In our own experience on the farside of the Moon, both Seth Byrne and I have witnessed UFOs. Despite the many thousands of verified and unverified sightings, until our discovery of the sphere, no one has ever come forth with a single physical example of a UFO. I do not believe in the reports that that extraterrestrial UFOs have crashed. Aliens who have the technology to travel between stars could certainly manage Earth's gravity. Yet now we have the physical evidence with the object we call the sphere, which was left on the Moon for us to find. From limited research we know that the object was not made by man. I would like to invite Dr. Zach Ulbricht to catch us up to date on what his team from the NASA meteorological labs have discovered about this object."

Zach's face appeared on screen and he thanked Kip. He showed a picture of the sphere. "Kip and Seth found this device on the floor of the Daedalus Crater over a year ago. They brought it to me while I was visiting Project Farside. I then took it with me to the NASA meteorological labs in Atlanta for scientific analysis. It is the most puzzling object that the NASA lab has ever attempted to analyze. Our lab has every analytical instrument known to science, yet other than its physical properties, we have only been able to study the surface and have learned little about the interior of this device except for the elements in its interior structure. The sphere is inert, hydrophobic, and does not react with chemicals. We tried to obtain a small sample but couldn't even scratch the surface with diamond tip tools or plasma cutters. It is impervious to every attempt to drill into it using lasers, acetylene torches, water jets, or even ion gas drills. The best we could do was to probe the interior with a high-power mass spectrometer. It is mostly made of platinum, indium, titanium, rhenium, and water. By weight water represented fifteen percent of the total mass. Until recently the sphere was solid and homogenous with all elements evenly distributed throughout. It is almost a perfect black-body radiator, meaning that it absorbs and emits almost all incident radiation. It assumes the temperature of any ambient surroundings. All I can tell you is that our science does not have the technology to further analyze the interior. We recently discovered that since we first measured its properties, the sphere began shrinking while retaining its original mass. We estimate if this shrinking continues at the present rate, in a few months it will be half of the original size yet still weigh in at 296.8 grams."

Kip thanked Zach and then resumed. "It is apparent that the aliens left this sphere. Seth claims it is 'a calling card.' The aliens knew that we would be unable to access the interior to learn much about it, so the question is why then did they leave it? Was it intended as a memento, or an example of their superior technology, or simply proof that they have visited? For centuries the ETs have been visiting. The Watchers have been incredibly careful not to reveal themselves or leave physical evidence behind. There is no doubt that they attempted to delay the start of LST observations by disrupting our spotter scope at the Annex. It is unclear what they intended to gain by this delay. They could have damaged the LST scope had they wanted to do so, but they only disrupted its calibration. Given the LST's extended abilities, they may have been concerned that astronomers might discover the home of the Watchers."

Kip continued. "Helen Luray is the Farside geologist who has been studying Goliath, an interstellar asteroid found on the floor of Daedalus. It may have a connection to our alien visitors and the sphere. Helen, could you tell us about Goliath?"

"Thank you, Kip," Helen responded and showed a picture of Goliath. "We were curious about this odd large asteroid that lay on the crater floor, so we visited it. There was no evidence of an impact crater or other evidence of its collision with the Moon. We named the asteroid Goliath and took samples from the surface and the interior to take back to the lab for analysis. Goliath is an iron-nickel-iridium asteroid with a unique mixture of other metals and isotopes. It is not a coincidence that the combination of elements and isotopes in Goliath is identical to that of the sphere, with the exception that the sphere does not contain isotopes. Like a fingerprint, the unique mixture of metals and isotopes indicates in which system the object formed and its age. Goliath is ancient and interstellar, a visitor that migrated from a solar system that is 32 light-years away. Significantly, Goliath is older than the formation of our own solar system. This information led our LST astronomer team to investigate the system designated as K34, a planetary system discovered fifty-six years ago by the Kepler project. The system's sun is about the same mass as that of our Sun, yet it is a billion years older and now grows hotter and larger as it enters the last phase of its long life. The K34 system contains five planets, two of which are rocky planets orbiting in the habitable zone. One of these planets designated K34c is about 10% larger than Earth and has an atmosphere of water, nitrogen, argon, carbon dioxide, and 18% oxygen. The presence of oxygen is significant because it proves that life must exist on this planet. I think we may have discovered a potential home of our alien visitors. If so, this begs the question of how these aliens from a system 32 light-years away are able to make a trip that even with an advanced technology would take them hundreds of years to complete."

Kip thanked Helen and opened the floor for online comments.

Dr. Francis Tammera offered a comment. "The alien technology may be one completely unknown to us. Since their solar system may be millions of years older than our solar system, it is not unreasonable to assume their civilization is also much older than ours and that they have developed a technology we have only dreamed about."

Dr. Smithers also commented, "The realization that our technology is inferior to that of aliens seems to intimidate some NASA managers, and for years they have refused to admit an alien presence on Earth, which would not be helpful in funding NASA request."

Dr. Eric Cobb from SETI offered his opinion. "We know that the speed of light imposes an absolute limit on a spaceship's velocity, so even assuming the aliens can achieve 30% of the speed of light, it would still take them over 100 years to travel to Earth. Perhaps 100 years is not such an impossible journey for beings who may live for centuries. In the days of whaling ships, a three- or four-year journey was not unusual, even for a sailor whose life span may have been less than fifty years yet would consider such a long journey practical. Alien spaceships have been observed by many credible folks, and I think they have been studying us for centuries. A few credible folks such as airline pilots have report seeing mother ships."

Pamela asked Eric, "Could humans really be so scientifically interesting that they would invest the time and money for such a long journey?"

"Perhaps the aliens think so," Eric said.

"Why do you think they tried to delay first light for the LST?" Pamela continued. "They have not interfered with our other telescopes."

"The LST on the backside of the Moon is the most advanced instrument we have to study exoplanets," Eric said. "They may have wanted to delay our discovery of their home planet, which now we may have done."

Dr. Francis Tammara opined, "The efforts to disrupt the LST still make no sense. Even if we know where the aliens call home, our technology poses no threat to them because we could not travel such a huge distance. More to the point, why did they leave the sphere for us to find?"

"Yes, that also is my question," Dr. Cobb responded. "For centuries, the aliens have taken care not to interact with humans or leave behind any physical evidence of their presence. I do not buy into the alien abduction stories or that their crafts have crashed on Earth. I also believe that due to the tremendous craft acceleration witnesses report, no living beings are on board. The so-called flying saucers must be drones."

Seth commented, "Yet now we have the sphere, direct physical evidence of their technology. Intelligent life and advanced technology are a process of biologic evolution that takes millions of years to develop. Goliath indicates that their system is much older than ours, so I think their civilization may be far older than ours and that they have developed a technology that we have not yet envisioned. To them we are an emerging species worthy of observation, but for some reason, they wanted to demonstrate their technology by leaving us the sphere."

Pamela commented, "Perhaps a message to warn us about how advanced they are, so stop searching for our home."

Dr. Cobb added, "It appears that we can expect the sphere will continue to shrink and become even more difficult to study. While we cannot sample the interior, we can probe it with our instruments like our Tetra sound probe. Initially the sphere appeared to be homogenous, but lately it has been gradually changing and stratifying into layers of various molecules and elements. Water has been migrating to the center to form a core of pure water. Some folks predict that it will continue to shrink beyond our ability to see it, but water is uncompressible and that will impose an ultimate diameter limit. I think it will stop shrinking when it attains the size of a tennis ball."

Dr. Smithers asked, "What physical process could cause this stratification and shrinking process?"

"That is a good question," Helen offered. "If the interior of the sphere is molten like Earth's interior, then stratification could take place as lighter materials migrate to the surface and heavier materials to the core. Yet the sphere's core is water, and the remainder is solid. As an object cools, it can shrink just like Earth has done. Nevertheless, there is no evidence that the sphere is cooling or loosing mass."

Zach said, "We are presently at a standstill with our investigation. Unless someone can come up with a new idea how to probe the sphere interior, we have discovered all there is to discover."

Kip asked if anyone else wished to comment, but no one else offered to weigh in.

"Then, I suggest that we conclude this video teleconference. Thank you all for attending and contributing to this forum."

With that the conference ended.

Chapter Fifteen
Aftermath

Two months after the Germain team returned from KARMA, Dr. Jio Zhongquin called Peter Perkins and said they would like to take them up on Dr. Germain's offer to visit Farside. Jio asked if a NASA shuttle could pick them up at KARMA. Peter spoke with Dr. Smithers and Seth and with their agreement told Jio they would arrange a shuttle from Horizon to pick them up next Tuesday. Dr. Jio Zhongquin, Dr. Xin, Dr. Lao Wong, and Peng, the optics technician, arrived on the shuttle in the Farside hanger where Peter, Seth, Pam, Dr. Chow, Vince, and Jim Karnowski were waiting to greet them. After cordial handshakes, Pam noticed that the technician was carrying a suitcase-sized black box. "What is in the box?" she asked Jio. "We have the optical bench with us," Jio said. "It is no longer working, and we hoped that your technicians could show Peng how to repair it."

Pam glanced at Jim and then said, "We will look at it. Dr. Karnowski can take it and Peng to our lab."

"It seems that we have uncovered the real reason for this visit," Chow whispered to Seth as they all walked to the elevator and took the one marked "Operations Center."

When they stepped out onto the platform that overlooks the Center, Sally Elmhurst was waiting and introduced herself as their guide. She led them into the L2 dining room where a meal had been prepared for them. After dinner and a brief tour of the facility, Sally took Dr. Chow and Peng back to the elevator and through the door marked "Observatory" where they were met by Dr. Hernandez and Jim who was an expert with the optical bench. They then took the optical bench to the lab and examined it with the alignment tools.

"There is actually nothing wrong with the bench; it is just not properly collimated for your telescope," Jim reported. "When I visited your observatory, I showed Peng the alignment process and made sure the optical bench was working properly. The bench is easily jarred out of alignment, so I assume this is what happened. I will show Peng how to collimate the bench."

Research continued at Farside for many years thereafter. Shortly after Dr. Zhongquin returned to KARMA, Dr. Smithers reassigned Dr. Perkins to a NASA management position back on Earth and appointed Dr. Pamela Hernandez as Project Farside director where she remained for ten years. Seth Byrne remained at Farside managing the LST until his time to return to Earth was up in 2069. Dr. Smithers appointed Seth as director of the Extremely Large Telescope (ELT) in Chile where he continued to discover other Kuiper Belt minor planets and refined the database on Janus.

Sequel

When I decided to write this novel, I had three objects in mind:

1. To acquaint the reader with the nearside of the Moon such that it was no longer the "dark side"

2. To provide a fanciful story to acquaint the reader with my guess how the tools of astronomy will have progressed in the next fifty years and the discoveries that these powerful machines might unveil

3. To provide some context and theories for the alien visitors that have been reported

9 781737 131434